CW01188770

QUEEN OF DECEPTION

EMPIRE OF SHATTERED CROWNS

1

MAY FREIGHTER

MOONLIT MOUNTAINS

ELISSE

ARCANE RIDGE

ILLERMONT

VINMARE

LEGIONARE'S FOREST

MAGE ASSEMBLY

ARCANE SEA

DRESGAN

GOSSET

MORGAN

GISNA

The Hollow Mountains
Northern Watchtower
Dragon's Heart Mine
Redford
Dragon Village
Grim Port
Newburn
The Royal Wood
Misty Sea
Port Lisza
Avonport
Heren
Drovia
Sinta
Avarea
Misty Peaks
Grenard
Vasa
Ashen Forest
Ponte
Crystal Sea
Reyniel
Setina

Copyright © 2023 May Freighter

All rights reserved.

ISBN: 979-8861538848

DEDICATION

To the love of my life who drives me crazy at times.

May we survive the trials ahead with sharpened blades and smiles on our faces.

FOREWORD

This book is written in U.K. English.

Some spelling may be different to the U.S.

Author's website:

www.authormayfreighter.com

Interior and Exterior Illustration:

Cristal Designs

CONTENTS

	Acknowledgments	i
1	The Cursed Princess	1
2	Her First Move	7
3	Regent	11
4	All About the Looks	19
5	Meeting with the Lords	24
6	The Lionhart Guild	35
7	Cold-Hearted Prince	49
8	Strange Hobbies	58
9	Restrictions	66
10	Upheaval	69
11	Not According to Plan	78
12	A Messy Situation	83
13	Decisions Decisions	87
14	Marquess' Arrival	98
15	Undertones	105
16	True Motives	112

17	Lives of the Fallen	115
18	Wiggling Baggage	119
19	Hand-Me-Downs	123
20	A Grande Secret	130
21	More Questions Than Answers	139
22	An Eventful Funeral	142
23	Reckless	152
24	The Lonely Queen	157
25	A Childhood Lost	163
26	House Escariot	170
27	A new Addition	177
28	Trust Issues	181
29	Wavering Support	192
30	Night Visitors	201
31	The Lower, The Better	206
32	Attack of the Beasts	209
33	About the Author	223

ACKNOWLEDGMENTS

I would like to thank my wonderful husband for suffering through this book and the following ones in the series. You have no idea how much I appreciate your feedback and ideas.

Also, a massive thank you to Nancy Zee from Crystal Designs for being my cover designer and proofreader. Although, you did a lot more than just proofread the novel, ha-ha. You are a great friend, and I cannot thank you enough!

And lastly, thanks to my editor for butchering my work.

"Who would have thought that dying once is not enough."
— Emilia V. Dante

1
THE CURSED PRINCESS

EMILIA

Winter, Year 608, Dante Kingdom

Swords clashing, guards shouting, and the commotion from the invasion of the Hellion Empire's soldiers could easily be heard from Emilia's tower.

Ever since she reincarnated into a fantasy novel she once read—The Cruel Empire—as a pitiful side character, Emilia was desperate to change her fate. She had staked everything on the ominous night when her character was destined to die.

For the past seventeen years, she knew the exact date when she and the rest of Dante's Royal Family would be slaughtered. Once she resigned herself to the new chance at living, she decided to change her fate. Years of sneaking around, planning, and waiting would finally pay off or lead to her demise.

Who knew that dying once is not enough?

Looking out of her bedroom window, she saw enemies encroaching on the entrance of the tower led by a blond man clad in mercenary attire. Her royal guards had long since abandoned their posts to protect the king. After all, she was the unneeded, "cursed" princess. Her sole value to her father was in her engagement to Count Bennett for an iron mine in the south.

Emilia sucked in a deep breath to soothe the brief influx of panic that had her hands trembling. She clutched the skirts of her worn-out dress. Once her breathing was under control, she plastered on a calm expression she had practised before a mirror. As she was not permitted to attend any balls or royal events, she had to rely on her only maid, Ambrose. She brought Emilia books and informed her of everything that went on in the palace until Emilia could build her network of people in secret.

The sound of heavy boots came to a stop outside of her door.

The wooden door swung open.

In the doorway, which suddenly looked too small, stood a man who would either become her saviour or her doom. Dressed in blood-splattered leather armour, his domineering posture was not overshadowed by his good looks or piercing glare.

She crossed her arms and tilted her head to one side. "I was getting tired of waiting, Your Imperial Highness."

Suspicion never left his green eyes, just like the grip on his sword did not loosen. "Are you the one who wrote that letter to me one year ago?"

"Of course. Who else do you think would bother to stay in this dusty old tower to meet the second prince of the great Hellion Empire?"

In his deep voice that rumbled from deep within his chest, he said, "From what I heard on the way here, you are Dante royalty, Princess Emilia. Or should I call you the Cursed Princess?"

Emilia wrinkled her nose at the ridiculous nickname given to her by the Church of the Holy Light. She had grown accustomed to it over the years, but hearing a possible ally utter it made her gut clench.

She kept her emotions in check. A single wrong word would

fulfil her destiny of being a headless corpse by the end of the night, along with the rest of Dante's royalty. "Your Highness, I have provided you with the perfect date for your coup," —which would have happened regardless of her involvement—"so now I wish to make a deal with you."

He raised a brow. "There is no benefit in keeping you alive. Instead of this pointless debate, I should drag you to the throne room and execute you along with your despicable family."

She swallowed her nerves. The bargain with the Devil had begun. "What if I help you take over this kingdom without needless bloodshed? Would that be enough to change your mind?"

"And how would you do that?"

She lowered her arms and moved to the small dessert table she had Ambrose bring in that morning. Two seats were available, and she took one of them before offering the opposite seat to the prince. "Please, join me."

The prince sheathed his sword and accepted her offer. He appeared too big for the chair as his muscular frame struggled to fit on her delicate furniture.

Up close, in the reflection of the dancing candlelight, she could see that he was much more handsome than the rumours said. The novel mentioned that his body was covered in scars from many years on the battlefield, but he managed to avoid getting his face cut. Because of that, he was not short on suitors back in the Empire. She couldn't help giving him a quick study. If she managed to get such a powerful man on her side, she could help him get the Empire's crown and be rewarded with the freedom she desperately craved. She may even ask for a small piece of fertile land to run an orchard.

"I thought we were going to discuss something…" His harsh tone startled her.

Emilia fished out an envelope from the pocket of her dress and pushed it across the table to him. As she removed her hand, she added, "This is the list of corrupt nobles who support my father."

He ripped open the envelope and unravelled the parchment inside. His eyes skimmed over the names. "What would you have me do with these nobles?"

"Since Your Highness is going to take over Dante, I suggest purging those who will be against you."

"This doesn't explain why I should keep you alive."

She smirked. "You are a smart man and, therefore, must know that it would be beneficial for a smooth transition of power if you allow me to live. I have secretly gathered the support of a third of the nobles while you possess the support of those who betrayed the king. If you were to kill me here, you would lose the support of my faction and have to deal with a civil war. Should you consider that to not be enough, I have also gained the trust of certain regions through charity work. Though, my brothers and father were not made aware of this." Her smile grew wider. "Thus, I have the support of key regions and nobles that I can offer you should we become allies."

The prince contemplated her words for a long moment. His poker face hid any hint at what was going on in that head of his, which shook Emilia's confidence in her gamble. "What do you want out of this?"

"A chance to prove I can be useful to you as well as freedom once you are crowned emperor."

He chuckled. "Dante is too small to be called an empire."

She did not waver and met his steely gaze. "I was not talking about Dante."

"You seem quite confident in your words."

"If I was not, would I have stayed here long enough for you to capture me?"

Everything she had said was the truth. She wanted Prince Thessian to become the next Emperor of Hellion because the alternative that awaited them was certain death.

After years of trying to figure out which prince she should side with, Thessian seemed like the best choice. The first prince, Cain, had everything. He built up a desolate fishing region of Hellios into a trading hub within five years of his instalment as the duke. There was nothing she could offer him that would make him protect her. The third prince, Kyros, would, eventually, take over the throne through dirty schemes and plots. She couldn't trust such a man not to stab her in the back one day. Her only choice was the second prince, Thessian. He respected loyalty and was trustworthy. As long as she didn't destroy the trust between them, she could live a carefree life.

He leant in, resting his weight on one elbow. "Very well, you have my attention, Princess. How do you plan to prove yourself to me?"

"I wish to temporarily rule Dante as regent while Your Highness is busy taking care of the important matters."

"I already have someone in mind for that position."

"Ah, yes, Marquess Walden. He is not suited for the job."

Thessian's face darkened. "I hope you are not slandering a good man's name for your own goals."

As he gripped the hilt of his sword, she quickly handed over a second envelope. "The proof is in there. See for yourself."

He opened the envelope and skimmed the contents inside.

Emilia struggled to not tap her foot in anticipation.

"Walden was receiving bribes from my brother?" Although he tried to act indifferent, the anger burning in his eyes was obvious. It would be for the best to never betray Thessian's trust. "How did you find this out when even my people could uncover nothing?"

"I have my ways." She rose from her seat and outstretched her hand to him in an offer of a handshake. "Do we have a deal, Your Highness?"

Thessian got up, towering over her like a marble pillar at the tallest temple. "Do not let me down, Princess."

They shook hands.

Emilia smiled. The hardest part was over, and she could move on to the next stage of her plan. "If you would excuse me, Your Highness, I wish to rest before the meeting with the lords tomorrow."

He seemed hesitant to leave but gave a curt nod and strode out of her chambers.

When she was positive he had left the tower along with his knights, she called, "Ambrose."

Ambrose was not just her maid. She was also a messenger to the Lionhart Guild.

The maid crept out of the false wall next to Emilia's bed. She had a plain look to not attract too much attention. "Send ravens to the lords. Tell them we have reached an agreement with Prince Thessian."

"Yes, Your Highness."

"Wake me in five hours and prepare a black dress. I must look like I am mourning."

She made her way to the bed, and Ambrose assisted her in removing her tattered dress.

After tonight, Emilia would no longer need to dress or act like a timid fool in front of others. Finally, she was on the path to freedom.

2

HER FIRST MOVE

THESSIAN

Outside of the tower, Thessian passed the envelopes to his second-in-command, Sir Laurence Oswald.

Without stopping, he ordered, "Verify the information in those documents as soon as possible and have someone sent to the princess to keep an eye on her."

Laurence seemed taken aback. "You are not going to kill her?"

"She has given me a reason not to." Thessian smiled to himself at the thought of how tough that young lady pretended to be in front of him when her body unconsciously trembled at the sight of his blade. "It will be interesting to see what she does next."

The palace guard had either been killed or subdued. Dante was considerably smaller than Hellion. Their resistance, too, was nothing compared to his capital. It was good fortune that his elite unit got into the castle without the need for a siege or the death of civilians.

The people of Dante had suffered under their king's heartless rule.

From the information Thessian collected before the coup, he learned that King Gilebert had raised the nation's taxes to the point where most peasants were dying outside of the capital. With the harsh and long winter, the harvest season had shortened, and the people were starving. He had seen more than enough suffering of the poor during the war. If he could unify the continent under Hellion's rule, perhaps the land and the people would one day be able to reach their full potential.

Upon arriving at the throne room where the bodies of the deceased king and his two sons lay in a pool of blood, he noticed the frightened servants that had been captured.

Laurence inquired next to him, "What shall we do about them, Your Highness?"

"Leave them to the princess. We will see what kind of person she is by the way she deals with them." Thessian waved for one of the knights in his unit to come over. He made a point to remember every name under his command. This time was no different. "Is this all of them, Cali?"

"We are making one final sweep of the castle, Your Highness," came her reply.

"Good. Make sure word of this coup does not leave these walls." Thessian glared at the servants who were whispering among themselves.

They immediately stopped and lowered their gazes.

Next, he made his way to the former king's office.

Gold and rare wood were used to decorate every nook and cranny. It was a sickening sight to see when the citizens starved for such opulent living. Even the throne room of such a small nation was decorated lavishly. Yet, the tower where Princess Emilia lived was barren of decorations or any valuables. The furniture was simple and plain. That girl's attire had been worn to the point where some threads had come out of the seams. He had to be blind to miss the way she was treated by her so-called family.

Despite that, her natural beauty wasn't lost on him. Her delicate features and penetrating blue eyes framed by long black hair made her pale skin seem almost ethereal.

Laurence walked to the king's desk and picked up a stack of papers that were left there. He scanned through them quickly. "Looks like the king was in the process of planning another ball for his sons. He had invited your brother, Prince Kyros, here for the festivities."

My brother again...

"What relation does Kyros have with King Gilebert?" Thessian rubbed his stubbly jaw in thought. He had no recollection of King Gilebert being invited to the palace by his father. Did they make an acquaintance after Kyros took over the Spiora duchy?

"My guess is their hobby of frivolous spending aligned," Laurence joked.

"According to the information the princess gave me, Kyros also has Marquess Walden in his pocket."

"That's odd. We couldn't uncover anything on the Marquess."

Thessian nodded. "That's why I need you to find out the truth. If she lied about the Marquess' involvement with my brother, I'll remove her."

Laurence's expression turned sour. "What if she didn't lie, and Walden has betrayed you?"

"Then we must secure the evidence of bribery and deal with him accordingly."

Laurence bowed. "I will start immediately, Your Highness."

Thessian sighed heavily. "How many times have I told you to call me by my name when we are alone?"

"As many as there are trees in the Fairview Forest."

"And you still won't do it?"

"Not unless it is a direct order, Your Highness."

Thessian glowered at his friend. Laurence knew full well that Thessian hated to order those close to him. He wanted them to work autonomously instead of following his every word.

"Get out of here before I punch you."

Laurence's laughter could be heard down the hall as he left for his new mission.

Beyond the window, dawn brightened the sky.

Ever since he received Princess Emilia's cryptic note about the perfect invasion date, he was amazed to see how easily things fell into place.

How could a confined princess orchestrate a coup of her kingdom to such an extent? Could she see the future? Or was there someone more powerful behind her?

For the moment, he could not place much trust in her. He needed to scrutinize every move she made. As he contemplated that, dozens of black ravens littered the sky.

He smirked. The princess has made her next move.

3
REGENT

EMILIA

Emilia woke to Ambrose's urging calls. She sat up in bed and stared at her hands while Ambrose fussed over the princess' attire for the day.

After being old enough to realize she had reincarnated in a new body and had a new family, Emilia taught herself the new language and made sure to hide her intellect and her old soul. It did not take long for her to find out that father did not want her and that her brothers were senseless bullies.

Now, at the age of seventeen, almost eighteen, Emilia could finally stop pretending to be a pushover. In the past, she had been used for her brothers' amusement, hated by the servants, and neglected by the king. The day had finally arrived when she could tear off her mask of misery and hold her head up high.

Mentally, she ticked off the things that had to be done as she climbed out of bed. Dealing with the lords would be the hardest part. There was no doubt in her mind that the lords who had supported her father's reign would not go down without a fight. In the meantime, she had to make it seem as though she was giving them the opportunity to side with her before removing their privileges. Otherwise, the unnecessary bloodshed would make her allies question her motives later on.

"Your Highness, shall I prepare a bath for you?" Ambrose asked.

"No need. Let us get started with today's schedule."

Ambrose inclined her head and wordlessly helped Emilia into a mourning dress they had ordered weeks in advance from a tailor. Then, she combed the princess' hair and skilfully organised the unruly ebony locks into an up-do with a few silver silk bands woven in.

Meeting Emilia's eyes briefly in the reflection of the mirror, Ambrose asked, "How would you like your makeup?"

"Regal but not celebratory."

Ambrose smiled and applied the cosmetics with utmost care.

"Are you that happy to be done with this tower?" Emilia inquired despite knowing the answer.

Her maid would no longer need to sneak in or hide out of sight when the head maid came around to check if the princess was still among the living.

Emilia was never supposed to leave her tower. The first time she escaped, she nearly broke her neck climbing down a makeshift rope in the middle of the night. Good thing she weighed next to nothing back then.

Once Emilia made some money, she bribed her drunkard guards with enough gold to live out the rest of their miserable lives comfortably. Not like her father paid them enough to care if she ran away in the middle of the night or died from starvation. The king's neglect was a great boon to her in that regard.

"I am refraining from shouting from the rooftops. Your Highness will no longer be forced to wear dresses that even the moths would not touch or hide your beautiful face."

Emilia grimaced. She knew full well how she looked to the point it hurt. During one of her trips, she caught a glimpse of her deceased mother's portrait. They were almost identical. After the queen died during childbirth, the king's hatred skyrocketed towards Emilia. Not only was she a useless princess, but she also killed the Queen of the nation. The ugly prophecy from the Church of the Holy Light added more fuel to the fire.

"It could not be helped. Appearances had to be kept, and my brothers had to see me as non-threatening or their torment would not stop at petty tricks."

"I wish I was with you from the start and protected you…"

"It would have made things harder."

Ambrose solemnly nodded.

Protecting someone requires power.

They both knew the harsh reality all too well.

The morning preparations took nearly an hour. By the time Emilia was ready to step into the palace for the first time in years, the winter sun was already warming the frostbitten ground.

Lastly, Ambrose donned a navy cloak embroidered with silver string onto Emilia's shoulders and put on a simple brown one on herself. "The air this morning is quite chilly, Your Highness."

"Thank you." Emilia smiled, and they left the tower through the door that led to the bridge that connected to the palace.

Outside, an unfamiliar female knight saluted Emilia. "Good morning, Princess Emilia. I am Dame Cali Louberte. I am here to escort you and be your guard on the orders of His Highness, Prince Thessian."

Emilia had anticipated a spy to be planted next to her by the prince. After all, there was no way he would trust her right away. She grabbed the knight's reddened hands and felt the chill through her gloved hands. This dame must have waited for quite some time for them in the cold. Cali was, indeed, dedicated to her duties.

Managing a bright smile, Emilia said, "I am looking forward to having such a beautiful knight protect me from harm." She glanced over her shoulder at Ambrose. "When we reach my father's office, please brew some hot tea for Dame Cali."

"I couldn't possibly. T-that would be extremely rude for me to do while on duty!" Cali turned beetroot red.

Emilia withdrew her hands and raised a dark brow. "Are you looking down on me, Dame Cali?"

Cali straightened her posture, taking on her military stance subconsciously as she folded her arms behind her back. "I wouldn't dream of it."

Emilia grinned. "I am glad. Please enjoy a hot drink without a guilty conscience. I could not possibly allow one of His Highness' people to suffer while they graciously care for me."

"Thank you, Your Highness," Cali replied along with a salute.

Emilia held back a chuckle. She hoped not all of Prince Thessian's people were so high-strung when dealing with her.

Passing through the halls of the royal palace, Emilia began to fully grasp how corrupt her father was.

The late king spent more money on appearances rather than helping restore his kingdom. Although she lived her past life in another world, selfish men like him existed there, too. They sold off their nation's territory or resources for profit while in office or betrayed the citizens who elected them into power by ignoring their promises.

In her previous life, her eidetic memory was a curse. She excelled at every subject she undertook, but the people around her hated her for it. One of her professors even claimed her thesis as his and published it as his research for peer review. Her parents, instead of siding with her, chose to blame her for the disgrace that brought them. They even asked her, 'Why would a highly-esteemed lecturer at the top university steal an undergraduate's thesis? You should think of a better lie if you didn't want to do the work.'

Her tears and frustration went unheard. Her parents were no better than the ignorant fool of a king she called 'Father' in this new life.

At the entrance to the throne room, Emilia spotted a knight who had accompanied Prince Thessian last night to her tower, talking to the guards stationed at the door. It was hard to see his face from above at that time. Now that she had the opportunity, she guessed he was Thessian's second-in-command, Sir Laurence Oswald.

According to the novel, Sir Laurence was Thessian's childhood friend and the third son of Marquess Oswald who protected the northern border of the Hellion Empire. Not only were the Oswalds loyal to the emperor, their family had accumulated quite a lot of influence in the military over the years. It was often mentioned in the story how Laurence's easy-going nature saved Thessian more than once during political events that the prince hated attending.

She produced a smile and greeted him, "Good morning. You must be Sir Laurence."

He finally took notice of her when the guards stiffened and stopped talking. With a single look at the princess, his eyes briefly widened, and he bowed in greeting.

The guards followed his example.

"Sir Laurence Oswald greets Her Royal Highness, The Flower of Dante, Princess Emilia." His chestnut-coloured hair, tied back with a red ribbon, oddly suited his handsome face. Without the bulky armour in the way, he seemed more approachable, too.

"Is this where the captured servants are being kept?"

"Yes. Do you wish to see them?"

Emilia nodded.

He made way for her to pass before following her into the throne room.

Emilia wasn't used to having an entourage. She glanced at Ambrose and Cali. "Give us some space."

The maid and the knight obeyed and stepped away from them.

Up ahead, Emilia noticed the drying blood marring the imported marble floor. The bodies of her brothers and father were covered with linen sheets. She was thankful she wouldn't need to see corpses before breakfast. Off to the right were the tied-up servants, some of whom were unconscious or sleeping.

The alert servants wearily watched her from under their lashes. She wondered what they thought of her now that she was no longer a person they could curse or insult. Their lives were in her hands, and the fearful expressions on their faces proved they had realised it.

Emilia approached the head butler of the palace, Sir Malcolm Rowell. She had rarely seen him as he only served the king. His grey mane of hair seemed to whiten overnight. The dark circles under his eyes and his gaunt appearance told her that he had not slept a wink.

"Sir Rowell, do you know who I am?" Emilia stared him down.

He swallowed nervously and lowered his head in greeting since he was already on his knees. "Your Royal Highness, Princess Emilia Valeria Dante."

"Very good," she replied sharply. "And whom do you serve?"

He hesitated after a glance at the dead bodies. "You, Your Royal Highness."

"I hope none of what has transpired will leave this room, Sir Rowell. Anyone found spreading rumours or gossiping about last night's events will be executed for treason." She glared at the servants for effect and raised her voice a notch. "Did I make myself clear?"

Sir Rowell lowered his forehead to the floor, which caused quite a commotion among the servants. He lifted his face just enough for her to see he meant every word. "We serve Her Majesty the Queen. Please permit this faithful servant to manage the household once more."

She nearly rolled her eyes. If he was as faithful as he claimed, he would have died along with his master. Yet, here he was, begging the new monarch for a chance to keep his job. No matter. He had the respect of the servants.

That was all she needed.

As long as he obeyed her orders, the others would fall in line. Over time, she could replace the staff with the people she trusted, but she didn't know how long she would remain in her role as queen.

Emilia softened her gaze. She borrowed a dagger from Sir Laurence and cut the butler's restraints.

"Please rise, Sir Rowell. Have the servants clean the throne room and arrange for the bodies of my father and brothers to be prepared for burial. We will hold the royal funeral in three days. Any guards who have died while executing their duties will need to be buried as soon as possible. Report to me when it is done."

"Yes, Your Majesty," Sir Rowell replied.

The servants kept their eyes on the floor as Emilia left them to be released by Laurence's men.

The tension in her shoulders slipped away when she stepped out of the throne room.

"I thought you would execute them." Sir Laurence's husky voice behind her made her jump. "Do you believe they will keep quiet about the coup?"

"Most of them value their lives more than gossip," Emilia said, facing him with her chin jutting out. "And those who dare speak out can easily be silenced. There is nothing to fear as long as we get the masses on our side."

He studied her intently which was beyond rude to someone of her status. In an instant, his carefree demeanour was replaced with open distrust. "I hope you realise that if you plan on using your newly acquired power against my master, I will gladly run my sword through you, *Your Majesty*."

She didn't waver. "My only goal is to help His Highness become emperor, Sir Laurence. I believe my actions from this moment forth will speak louder than words."

"I'm looking forward to seeing them." His pleasant mask returned, and he bowed and backed away as Ambrose and Cali came into view.

The prince's second-in-command could not be underestimated. He was a good man and a loyal subject, according to the novel, who died alongside Thessian in the end. To help Thessian, she needed to get close to him, which meant she had to get Laurence's approval. The weight of the future rested on her shoulders. Although she had saved herself from pointless death, she had to keep the Hellion Empire from falling into Prince Kyros' hands. To do that, she had only three years left. After all, the hero of the story would not appear until after Prince Kyros became a tyrant emperor.

"Are you feeling unwell anywhere, Your Highness?" Ambrose asked.

"I'm fine." Emilia shook off the remnants of her worries. "From now on, call me 'Your Majesty', Ambrose."

4
ALL ABOUT THE LOOKS

THESSIAN

Thessian had spent all night reading through the documents in the king's office and burning through multiple candles. To get comfortable, he had removed his leather armour and sat on the king's cushioned chair. He rubbed his tired eyes when the morning sun filtered through the arched windows.

There was a knock on the door, and Thessian shouted, "Come in."

Laurence walked into the room with a mischievous grin. Whatever his friend was up to, Thessian did not wish to be a part of it.

Laurence stopped a short distance away from the desk and leaned his side against the intricate wall panelling. He pulled out an apple that he rubbed against his trouser leg and bit into it. "I did not think you were the type to fall for beauty, Your Highness."

Frowning, Thessian raised his head from the paperwork. "What are you talking about?"

"I met Princess Emilia. It was no wonder she was kept in a tower. Few women on the continent could be compared to her."

Thessian realised what Laurence was implying. "I did not let her live because she was pretty."

"No. Of course not." Laurence took another juicy bite, making Thessian's stomach rumble. He had not eaten since yesterday's supper.

Pretending to act disinterested, Thessian resumed his reading. "What did she do?"

"She got the head butler to acknowledge her as the new queen and freed the servants. Do you think we should stop her?"

"No. Let her do as she pleases. We will return to camp once we are done here."

Laurence stopped chewing and swallowed loudly. "She could turn the nobles against us."

"The princess knew when the coup was going to happen. She could have easily fled the castle. Instead, she remained and even struck a deal with me." Thessian rested his chin on his fist. "I think we should observe her a while longer."

"Very well." Laurence pushed away from the wall. "As long as you are not secretly planning a wedding behind my back."

Thessian glared at him. Not only was he hungry, but his friend's idiotic remark also struck a nerve. He had no time to contemplate marriage when he was busy trying to win the position of crown prince. "If you are done spouting nonsense, go get me the answers I asked for last night."

"Yes, yes." Laurence produced a dramatic bow and sauntered out of the office with a skip in his stride.

Thessian shook his head. Emilia was ten years younger than him. She was still a child. Although she did not behave like one, she probably secretly wanted to attend balls, dance with suitors, and go to tea parties like the other ladies her age.

Not long after, Emilia entered the king's office, followed by a maid and Dame Cali, and stopped in her tracks. She gave a nod of her head. "Greetings, Your Highness. I did not expect you to be here this early."

He rose from his seat and gave her a proper greeting in return. "I saw your ravens not too long ago. You have begun your work quite early as well."

Emilia smiled and then spoke over her shoulder. "Ambrose, have the chef prepare a meal for me and His Highness. Dame Cali, follow her and do as I have asked this morning."

The maid wordlessly left the room, but Cali glanced at Thessian for secondary approval before complying.

"How did you know I was hungry?" he asked.

"There is no servant here to look after your needs and no traces of you eating."

Her answer amused him. "You are quite observant, Your Majesty."

A bit of rose flushed her cheeks at the mention of her new title. "Thank you kindly."

"Shall we make our way to the dining room?"

Thessian escorted her to their destination. Standing next to him, Emilia appeared small and fragile. The top of her head barely reached his shoulder. Unlike Laurence, Thessian never had a sister and hardly spent any time with the ladies during the banquets and balls. Aside from the common courtesy, he was not sure what to talk about with women. Surely, she would find talk of military tactics or troop management boring.

Thessian waited for her to be seated by a nervous servant before he took his seat opposite her at the table. With a wave of her hand, she dismissed the servants.

"Being in a room alone with me will have the servants wagging their tongues to no end," he told her.

She met his eyes as she draped a napkin over her wrist. "At least, they will be less inclined to talk about last night."

"Now that you are Queen, what do you plan to do?"

"I plan on getting as many nobles as possible to side with us. The ones who will not submit will need to be replaced." She folded her hands on her lap but kept her steady blue gaze on him. "Before the year's end, I would like to help the citizens by passing laws to regulate working hours and breaks. I do not wish to be like the late king who allowed the lords to work their people to their graves." Her expression brightened when she began discussing further improvements to the kingdom's infrastructure and education as well as the eventual abolition of serfdom and slavery. A moment later, she caught herself. "What are your thoughts?"

"Did King Gilebert hire private tutors to teach you?"

"No. I learned from the books my maid secretly brought me from the royal library."

He doubted any child could understand such complex topics with a mere maid there to help them. Was Emilia secretly a genius? If so, her father had greatly underestimated his daughter's potential. Yet, she could also be lying to him, though he did not see the benefit in her doing that.

"It seems you are sceptical of my abilities. I can recite every book I have ever read word-for-word. Feel free to test me. Even better, you could pick a book from the library and let me read a page."

Does she have a perfect memory? To hide his surprise, he cleared his throat.

Thankfully, to save him from further embarrassment, her maid, Ambrose, arrived with servants in tow with their meal. The silver plates were placed in an orderly fashion and the silverware was carefully organised. Next to him, a maid poured a goblet of wine for him that would go well with the seasoned lamb loin. A selection of cheeses and bread were placed between him and Emilia. Dante Kingdom's food appeared mundane compared to the variety often seen in the empire. He did not mind all that much. On the battlefield, the rations were a lot worse than what was in front of him. He made a point to eat the same food as his troops because they were like a family to him.

"Have you recalled a good memory, Your Highness?"

He raised his head. "Was I being that obvious?"

"Somewhat."

The rest of the meal passed over a pleasant conversation about pointless things like the cold weather and the differences in their customs. He assumed she did not want to discuss anything of importance in front of the servants, so he played along. His gut feeling told him that she would be a great asset in the future. He did not regret sparing her life. After all, Laurence may have cursed him to his grave for depriving the world of another beauty.

5
MEETING WITH THE LORDS

EMILIA

Emilia was pleasantly surprised by how easy it was to talk to Prince Thessian. In the novel, he seemed reserved with nobility and only showed his real personality to those serving with him in the military. He was a character she resonated with the most, because she, too, used to wear a mask for the outside world, be it at her university, home, or during her part-time job. She couldn't recall having any friends that mattered to her in her past life. The same could be said about her current predicament. Just like before, she could trust in no one but herself. Thessian may find her interesting to talk to at that moment, but no one knew what tomorrow would bring. He could suddenly change his mind and behead her.

Thessian left right after the meal, allowing her to visit the king's office. She searched her father's desk, finding the king's seal in one of the drawers. With it, she could write and validate royal decrees until the blacksmith forged her seal.

She got down to work, producing letter after letter to the most influential lords on her list, informing them of the king's and princes' passing along with the date for the funeral. She wrote a letter addressing the masses that would be heralded at town squares about the changes with as much feigned regret as she could muster, embellishing some details, like how valiantly the princes tried to defend the king or how the attack came from a group of traitorous nobles. She left the names out to give the king's faction a chance to take her side. It was a good way to rid the kingdom of the nobles who once supported the king's terrible rule. Undoubtedly, some of them would attempt to flee, which could play in her favour as such a move could be seen as suspicious by the public.

To each of her father's supporters, she wrote a letter with her demands. They could either flee or pledge their allegiance to her. From the information she had gathered, the king's faction was corrupt beyond all hope. Most of them would choose to flee. The three she was most concerned about were Duke Anatole Malette, Marchioness Lucienne Durand, and Marquess Louis Sardou. They owned large territories with sizeable armies. According to her investigation, if they joined hands to start an uprising, she could lose without proper military backing.

I have to find a way to divide them.

Her head began to hurt. She looked at Ambrose, who immediately perked up. "Could you make some tea for me?"

The maid curtsied and backed out of the room.

Before long, Sir Rowell arrived. He bowed low and entered the room with Emilia's permission.

"Have you completed the tasks I've assigned, Sir Rowell?"

"Yes, Your Majesty. The bodies of the late king and two princes were sent to the chapel for preservation, and the guards who lost their lives are being buried as we speak. I have made a point to speak to the servants once more about spreading needless gossip. The Head Maid and I will keep a close eye on the servants in the coming weeks. Those who utter a single word of last night's events will be whipped in front of the others."

Emilia did not like the Head Maid Tamara Hester. That woman often supported the princes' antics in tormenting Emilia. "I see. Keep me updated."

"Certainly, Your Majesty. May I make a suggestion?"

"Speak."

"You need to pick some ladies-in-waiting from the nobility. This will help you raise your influence as well as unburden your personal maid."

"You have a point," Emilia agreed. "Do you have anyone in mind?"

"I wouldn't be presumptuous enough to think my opinion would be of great value."

She sat back in her seat and folded her arms over her chest. "Not one lady comes to mind, Sir Rowell? I may have spent my life in the tower, but I have heard you advised my father in private on the matters of nobility. As a highly respected man who served the crown for more than twenty years, I would think your opinion weighs more than that of a common noble."

The tips of his ears turned bright red. The head butler liked being praised, it seemed.

Sir Rowell cleared his throat. "Thank you for your kind words, Your Majesty. It may not be a bad idea to include Lady Christine Durand, the third daughter of Marchioness Durand. She has been unsuccessful at the balls because of her plain looks and lack of interest in marriage."

The Marchioness was one of the people Emilia was contemplating turning to her side. Destroying the possibility of the three most powerful families in the kingdom working together against her coincided with her plans. She couldn't stop a smile from stretching her lips. The butler was more cunning than she had anticipated. He lived up to the title of the King's Shadow. "Send an invitation to Marchioness Durand. I would like to meet with her sometime next month."

Emilia had to tread with great caution as Marchioness Durand had got a lot of help from Duke Malette and his wife in her business ventures. Receiving favour from the new monarch could sway the tide just enough for Emilia to forge cracks in their relationship. For now, she needed more information on their weaknesses and business affairs.

"Sir Rowell, I hope you would submit a list of suitable candidates as soon as you are able." As an afterthought, she handed him a list of nobles who were due to arrive at the palace. "Inform me once everyone on this list is present and escort them to the throne room."

"Will do, Your Majesty." He excused himself.

By the time Ambrose arrived with tea, Emilia had long since forgotten she was thirsty. She needed more information on those three major houses of the Dante Kingdom. If Marchioness Durand could be flipped to her side, Emilia could then focus on dismantling the influence Duke and Duchess Malette had on society.

As she sipped her tea while looking out the window at the frost-bitten greenery in the garden below, she ran multiple scenarios through her mind.

Taking her eyes off the dull view, she moved to her desk to write a letter to the Lionhart Guild that was located at the back of the bustling Market Street of Newburn. Guild Master Lionhart had been her business partner since she was nine. Sneaking out of the palace as a child was hard. By the time she found the guild based on the author's loose description, the city guards nearly caught her.

Upon their first meeting, she gave Lionhart enough important information about a certain kingdom's territory changes and some mine locations, and they made great investments. In the following years, he became less sceptical of her wild claims and followed her investment suggestions without protest. With a cut of thirty per cent, she was no longer short on money and had the guild at her disposal, as well as the friendship of the guild master. Though, to that day, she didn't know his past or real name. From their meetings, she assumed he was a disgraced noble from another nation as dark skin was quite uncommon in the Dante Kingdom.

In her letter, she asked for new information on the Marchioness Durand's and Duke Malette's families. She also asked for a meeting with Lionhart to be scheduled for that night. As much as she wanted to rest after a long day, she had a goal that needed to be achieved.

Emilia sealed the letter with wax and handed it to Ambrose. "You know where this goes."

Ambrose shoved the letter into the inner pocket of her maid's uniform and backed out of the room with her head bowed.

From where Emilia stood, she noticed Cali's eyes following Ambrose. She smiled. "I would send you with her, but I fear I require a guard for my next appointment."

Emilia checked the time on the wrought-iron clock on the mantelpiece. It was almost five. Her supporters were already arriving at the palace. Sir Rowell was right. Some ladies-in-waiting would come in handy when managing her schedule and events in the future. It would unburden Ambrose who had to do everything for Emilia to date.

Emilia glimpsed her appearance in a silver hand mirror in the desk drawer and steeled herself for the meeting. The nobles were going to pester her with their needs and demands. Their support wasn't cheap.

The majority of the lords, who would be waiting for her, were loyal to a point. They expected to be rewarded, but she had no intention of using the kingdom's gold to please them. Land and titles were the only things she could use to keep them on her side. A handful of those who supported her reforms and ideals would be among them. One of them was Count Baudelaire. He owned a sizeable chunk of land next to Marchioness Durand's territory and had a flourishing trading relationship with the nobles because he owned most of the kingdom's vineyards. He cared for his people, and they paid back with hard work in return. In the future, Emilia didn't want more people to die from over-working like Ambrose's father.

Her gaze was drawn to Cali who wore an unmarked mercenary armour. Letting Cali guard Emilia in front of the nobility in that attire would bring unneeded questions. "Cali, find Sir Rowell and change into the royal guard's uniform."

The knight was visibly confused by the order but left the room without protest.

Finally alone, Emilia folded her hands behind her head and stretched.

"My God, this feels so good!" Using proper posture all day long was a different kind of torture. She was stiff in places she didn't know had muscles. She may as well make a talking puppet with her appearance to use during long meetings. She giggled. The nobles would probably faint if they saw a robot or run away screaming about forbidden magic.

Ah well...

The knock on the door forced her to resume her regal posture and indifferent expression. "Yes?"

Sir Rowell entered the room. "Your Majesty, your guests have arrived and been escorted to the throne room."

"What about Dame Cali? Did she receive a new uniform?"

"I've sent her to find a spare uniform in the barracks and will have a new one made for her this week. She will wait for you in front of the throne room once she has changed. In the meantime, you should let the lords wait while you gather your thoughts. After all, the Queen is always on time while everyone else is simply early."

She smirked. "I'm starting to like you more and more, Sir Rowell."

Emilia made her entrance into the throne room to the announcement of the herald. Five steps behind her, Sir Rowell and Dame Cali followed. With as much grace as her body could produce, she sat on the throne and rested her hands on the armrests. One look at the bowing lords was enough to know that some had not been happy about the wait. Those particular nobles, she committed to memory.

"Thank you all for coming here on such short notice."

"It is a pleasure to be summoned here by Your Majesty," Count Baudelaire announced from the front row.

The others mumbled their agreement.

Emilia couldn't help her smile. Count Edmund Augustine Baudelaire was not a tall man. His grey mane of hair was combed towards the back of his head where his locks were beginning to thin out. Unlike many other nobles, his steel-coloured eyes shone with sincerity. The only way she convinced him to join her side was by exposing her plans for the kingdom's reforms. He was not a fan of her father and disliked the two princes. So, when they met in secret for the first time, the eyes that now reflected possibilities were filled with doubt and suspicion.

"Lord Baudelaire, it has been a while."

"Indeed, it has, Your Majesty." His smile was almost hidden behind his bushy moustache. "I look forward to seeing the changes we talked about."

There it is—a subtle hint that he will hold me accountable if I break my word.

She raised her voice and met the multiple gazes of the curious nobles. "Once the assignment of my ministers is complete, I would like your input on the best way to lead the Dante Kingdom. We cannot continue to tax our people into endless debt or out of their farmlands. Every one of the citizens is the heart of Dante and with your help, my dear lords, I wish to build a strong foundation for our home that will last for centuries to come."

Her speech was followed by roaring applause. Pleased with their response, she moved on to granting their rewards for supporting her. Before becoming Queen, she had made deals with those who needed to be nudged into giving her their help. Most wanted a bit of land for themselves. Since the king hoarded plenty of territory, she had no reason to refuse. Deciding on the ministerial positions would have to wait as she needed more time to choose. Aside from Count Baudelaire for the position of Prime Minister, she was at a loss. Scheduling an appointment with him to decide on key positions after her coronation wouldn't be a bad idea.

Once the time came to grant new titles, she looked to Sir Rowell who came over with the ceremonial sword. He bowed low as he offered the sheathed weapon to her. The scabbard, encrusted with priceless, crimson jewels and coated in gold, seemed just like the previous ruler—showy and pompous. The golden hilt looked like it was made for show and not to be handled due to its bulkiness.

She stifled a sigh and commenced the boring process of granting titles and higher ranks.

As she was about to finish up, the door to the throne room burst open. She spotted the herald at the door who was at a complete loss of what to do behind the intruder.

Emilia clenched the hilt in her hand, nearly cutting the kneeling baron's neck with the blade. She lowered the sword as Duke Malette approached the throne, not once stopping to greet her or show respect.

The duke was stopped by Sir Rowell who blocked him midway. "Your Grace, have you forgotten all manners on the way here? You are in the presence of Her Majesty the Queen."

"How can that child become our queen? She lived her life in an isolated tower and hasn't even learned how to read or write. What qualifications does a girl like that have to rule a kingdom?" Duke Malette snapped back, each word louder than the last.

Emilia maintained her composure. The rule of the court was the same as in an argument. The person who lost their temper first was on the losing end. "If I recall correctly, my father took up the throne at the age of sixteen." She dismissed the baron and resumed sitting on her throne with the sword still grasped in one hand. "As for my writing and reading capabilities, believe me, there are no issues. I mastered all languages on the continent at the age of eight and memorised every book in the Royal Library last fall. Could you say the same?"

Duke Malette scrunched up his red face. "You must be lying to all these—" He scanned the nobles present, probably taking in the fact that only a fraction of the nobility was present. He grinned. "Are these the traitors who helped you stage a coup?"

The nobles in the room fired back at him for suggesting something utterly preposterous.

Sir Rowell was ready to speak when Emilia silenced him. She ignored the duke and said to the nobles, "Our business is concluded for today. I thank you for coming."

The nobles shuffled out of the room, muttering to each other under their breaths.

Emilia was sure of a couple of things. First, Duke Malette had a spy in the palace. His territory was quite far—two days' ride by carriage from the capital. That meant the spy left to inform him of Thessian's attack as soon as it began, taking the fastest horse in the stables, it seemed. Second, the Duke wanted the king to die. He could have reached out to the nearby marquess for immediate military support but didn't. The duke was no fool. He saw these events as an opportunity.

"Will you continue to behave like a fool now that the audience is gone?" she asked calmly.

Duke Malette attempted to get past Sir Rowell, but the knights took their swords out in warning.

"You may speak from there, Your Grace."

Begrudgingly, he gave the briefest bow in the history of the royal family. "I humbly request to speak with Your Majesty in private."

Had he not been the only duke in Dante, Emilia would have beheaded him for such an obvious insult. She motioned for the guards to sheathe their weapons. "Here is as good a place as any, unless you do not trust the palace guards or the head butler?"

"Very well." He glowered at Sir Rowell one last time until the head butler stepped to one side and stopped blocking the duke's view of the throne. "I came here as soon as I heard the news of what happened. It boggles my mind that the intruders spared a wenc—a princess when they came here for the royal family."

"Who are these intruders you speak of? My father and the two princes were killed by the traitorous lords who wished to claim the throne for themselves." She placed her hand over her chest and faked sadness to the best of her ability. A few more seconds, and she squeezed out a tear. "My brothers valiantly fought them off but died from fatal wounds. By the time I was informed of what happened at the palace, the traitors fled."

"Based on your story, the traitors were quite stupid," Duke Malette grumbled.

"I agree. They must have forgotten about my existence as it was never of any importance to the king, which is why I am here today."

One glance at his face told Emilia that he didn't believe a single word. Without proof, he had to take her at her word as her station was above his. Aside from the spooked spy who could identify a couple of the attackers, the duke had nothing. No one would expect Hellion Empire's troops to invade Dante and leave the kingdom in the rightful hands of the princess. The story about the traitorous lords, while far-fetched, was more believable. Now, she just needed to make evidence that suited her needs and remove the opposing nobles.

Pursing his lips, Duke Malette rubbed his grey-streaked beard. "Did Her Majesty truly memorize every book in the Royal Library?"

"Do you think I would lie about something like that?"

His burning gaze raked her expression for any signs of nervousness. "Not at all. I only wish to point out that being book smart and having real-world experience are not the same thing."

"I am well aware, which is why after the king's funeral, I will speak with the lords and ask for their guidance." Before he could counter her, she added, "As I am yet uncertain of who killed my father, I am weary of trusting the nobles I am not acquainted with."

"It is good we became acquainted today, Your Majesty."

"Yes. It is." Emilia needed him to tell her what he actually wanted. From his stiff posture, he wasn't willing to do so in the throne room.

Could there be another spy?

She noted that a few of the guards were originally from the palace guard. They were mixed in with Thessian's men. She doubted Duke Malette had personal dealings with Thessian to recognise his knights on sight. In conclusion, one of the guards had the possibility of being a spy for another noble. She needed a huge rake to weed out all the eyes and ears around her. Had the king not died by Thessian's hand, he would have perished from stupidity.

He was lucky Sir Rowell stuck around and removed most of the threats. But if another guard was a spy, she needed to get rid of him before he spilt the beans.

"Sir Rowell," she called.

The head butler approached her and lowered his head enough for her to whisper in his ear. "Identify every guard in this room and who introduced them. Ignore Prince Thessian's men. Make sure to collect all of their outgoing correspondence without them knowing."

The butler retreated to one side after she handed him the ceremonial sword.

"Lord Malette, it is getting late, and I am tired after a long day. How would you like to use one of our guest rooms? We can speak more tomorrow."

"That sounds perfectly fine, *Your Majesty*." Her title coming out of his lips sounded like it was dragged through every chamber pot in the castle.

She left the throne room through the side door. With Cali on her heels, Emilia asked, "What did you think of the duke?"

"He was extremely rude, Your Majesty."

"I don't want to hear the diluted version of your thoughts."

"Then, had I been in Your Majesty's position, I would have stabbed him with the sword enough times to make him resemble a pin cushion or forced him to eat his toupee in front of others."

Emilia let out a hearty laugh, which she soon converted into a ladylike giggle for the sake of keeping up appearances. It was a good thing Cali wasn't in her shoes, or the palace servants would deem their queen not only cursed but also crazy. Though, it was nice to know she wasn't the only one thinking of poking the duke full of holes.

6
THE LIONHART GUILD

EMILIA

Evening fell upon the kingdom, and Emilia watched the captivating view of snowfall from her new bedchambers in the palace. She had a lot more space to move around in and the furniture did not look like it was robbed from some poor noble's storage shed.

Yet, the luxurious setting did not bring her any joy. She thought that once she escaped the tower, she could finally breathe freely. So, why hadn't that happened? Why did she feel like she was more bound to the palace than ever before?

Was it a mistake to become regent?

She shook her head as she stepped away from the window. The man Thessian entrusted the Dante Kingdom to in the novel later betrayed him because Marquess Walden was working for the third prince. Saying outright to Thessian that the man he trusted was about to sow dissent without evidence would have left her without a head. She had to give him hints and nudge him towards making his conclusions about his younger brother. Otherwise, Thessian may start to doubt her every word.

Emilia heard light footsteps outside of her room followed by four soft, intermittent knocks. That was the signal Ambrose and Emilia came up with when they began working together.

Emilia took a seat on a plush settee in front of the marble fireplace with her hands neatly arranged in her lap. "Come in."

Ambrose snuck in. Her eyes grew wide momentarily at the expensive furnishings, just as Emilia's initially did when Sir Rowell escorted her there.

"What do you think?" Emilia asked, grinning. "This room could pay for an entire town's salaries for a month."

"Indeed, Your Majesty." Ambrose did not find the situation as amusing as Emilia. Perhaps that was due to Ambrose's and her sister's upbringing in the slums. After their father died in the mines, and their mother came down with a serious illness, the children were left to their own devices. According to Ambrose, she was only eleven when she had to look after her six-year-old sister. A year later, without proper care and medicine, their mother followed their father to the afterlife, which was when they were taken to an orphanage that Emilia supported in secret. During one of Emilia's visits when she was twelve, she found Ambrose in the backyard, staring blankly at an open book. At first, Emilia thought the girl was engrossed in reading only to find that the book was upside down. In fact, Ambrose had no idea how to read or write. That night, Emilia decided to hire Ambrose as her personal maid as she could not shake the look of stubbornness on Ambrose's face. Since then, Emilia promised to look after Ambrose and her sister, Ivy, as long as Ambrose served her to the best of her ability.

"I apologise, Ambrose," Emilia said, curving her lips into a weak smile. "That was insensitive of me."

The girl bowed at the waist. "Your Majesty, it was my mistake to let my emotions show. I will work harder!"

Emilia's fingernails dug into her palms. Ambrose was the only person entirely on Emilia's side in the whole Dante Kingdom, and yet the maid didn't know that Emilia came from another world or that they were characters in a fantasy novel someone once wrote.

Does it matter?

This was Emilia's second chance at life as someone else. This time, she might get to live past her twenties, if luck stayed on her side.

Blowing out a heavy breath, Emilia asked, "Did you set up a meeting?"

"Yes. Mister Lionhart will wait for you in his secondary office." From under her cloak, Ambrose produced a sack with Emilia's disguise.

"Good." Emilia got up and started to remove her dress. "And what about Dame Cali?"

"I sent her on an errand. She should be away for another ten minutes."

Once out of her stuffy dress, Emilia ordered, "Take off your clothes and pretend to sleep in my bed. I've prepared a wig for you in case you need to look like me." Although Ambrose was two years older than Emilia, they had similar build and height. In the dark of the night, telling the two of them apart would be difficult. "I'll slip out through the secret passage."

Ambrose quickly stripped to her chemise and crawled into the canopied, curtained bed where she put on the black wig.

Emilia hurriedly slipped on her commoner's disguise. "What do you make of Cali?"

"She is a trustworthy lady with a good heart."

"Why do you think that?"

"I have taken the initiative to speak with her as much as I could today," Ambrose admitted from behind the curtain. "She is chatty, but has revealed nothing about Prince Thessian or Sir Laurence."

Emilia secured the cloak around her neck with a simple silver clasp, and she was finally done looking like a short, lanky man. She tied her hair with a ribbon and shoved it inside her hood. "I doubt Laurence would allow a blabbermouth into the elite ranks."

"There is something else I have observed…"

"Oh?"

"Dame Cali is extremely fond of Sir Laurence."

Emilia rubbed her chin in thought. "It would be best to avoid sharing anything we don't want Laurence to know. After all, love can cause a serious case of the loose-tongue disease."

"Is that a real thing, Your Majesty?"

Trying not to laugh, Emilia replied, "Of course. Would I lie to you?"

"Then I best never fall in love as I would like to serve you for as long as I live."

Emilia pulled on the nearby wall-mounted candleholder. The fire in the fireplace instantly died as a secret passage behind the fireplace opened.

She grabbed hold of a lantern she had prepared in advance. "You can fall in love, Ambrose. You're just not allowed to be a blabbermouth." As an afterthought, she added, "When an assassin shows up, try not to hurt him too much."

Emilia's secret passageway led to the heart of the catacombs. The tunnels spanned the entirety of the castle, with multiple intentional dead ends designed by a rather paranoid grandfather of King Gilebert. Not that Emilia blamed the guy for wanting a way out of his stronghold to meet with the peasant girls under the cover of the night. The late monarch had an entire section of the Royal Library dedicated to his sexual exploits. In one of those ghastly reads were the blueprints for the passageways. Hopefully, the later kings did not mess with the plans.

The sound of her booted feet was drowned out by a burst of squeaks from one of the dark tunnels. Emilia stilled and gripped the hilt of her dagger under her cloak. She hated rodents. The princes often startled her by letting a handful of rats loose in her tower. She nearly fainted from horror when one of those nasty beasts climbed onto her bed.

She shuddered at the memory and picked up her pace. The faster she got out of those tunnels, the faster she could breathe in air that didn't smell like someone's rotting coffin. Compared to the modern cities in her past life, giving Dante's capital, Newburn, the title of "city" was excessive. The population was almost seven thousand. At least, that was the information provided during the last census.

Nearly twenty minutes later, and with her mind firmly sticking to the pointless statistics she read in the past, Emilia emerged through one of the metal gates well outside of the palace walls. She ended up in the small hunting woods that the royalty liked to use for entertainment. Aside from foxes and game brought by the nobles for the king's amusement, no wild animals of note dwelled there.

She made her way to the cobbled road that joined Newburn's Main Street and Market Street at a large obelisk. Most of the houses there had a half-timbered, Gothic design with a shop on the ground floor and living quarters on the first floor. The pointed roofs made them seem like triangular cheese slices.

Peeking from under her hood, she saw first-hand how lifeless the eyes of her subjects were. Lionhart once told her that the capital's people represent the state of the nation. Happiness and pride often meant that the citizens were prosperous in most of the land.

Sadness and despair appeared in war-torn countries. If what he said was true, the rest of Dante was hell. King Gilebert let the nobles do as they pleased as long as they paid their taxes on time. His greed was the cause of his people's suffering.

Emilia wasn't expecting to be on the throne for long. Her main goal was to help Thessian become emperor, so she could get her plot of land and live off the sales of her goods—a quiet and fulfilling life.

Her stride faltered when she saw a scrawny child begging outside of a tavern for scraps. She couldn't save everyone. Those people would throw mud or dung at her if they knew her real identity.

Closing her heart to the misery around her, she hurried to the guild's back door that to the naked eye appeared like a fortune-telling tent. One of the younger guild members, Ernesto, liked to dress up as a foreign woman with mystical powers. Magic on the continent was rare, so the common folk had never seen it in action. To them, a few on-point observations coupled with chance guesses from Ernesto—or Estina in today's case—were equally as good as a magical ability. In the novel, the most influential mages were the hero and Prince Kyros' advisor. That advisor was part of the reason why things went so swimmingly for Prince Kyros in his attempt to steal the empire's throne.

"Want to know your fortune, sir?" Ernesto asked in a well-practised, feminine voice. "I can tell you when you'll meet your true love."

"No need. I had my palm read yesterday," she replied with the passphrase.

Ernesto lifted his head and grinned a toothy smile. Multiple of his teeth had been replaced with metal crowns. In the dull lamplight of his fortune-telling tent, his teeth looked like they were melting in his mouth. "It's been a while, Lady Em. Please go to the back, as usual."

Emilia nodded and proceeded inside. Ernesto was one of the newcomers who joined the guild in the last three years. His circumstances were unusual enough for Lionhart to personally bring the young man. For some reason, neither Ernesto nor Lionhart wished to share the details with her. Not like it mattered in the grand scheme of things. She was merely curious enough for the subject to pop into her head occasionally.

She entered the guild through the back door. Nothing had changed in that place. It smelled of cheap alcohol and cigarettes. The green paint on the wooden panels, or what was left of it, had permanently changed colour to two shades darker. There was no seating or art to examine on her way to the end of the storage room. The only light in the room came from a single lantern that hung near the entrance, covering the rest of the space with haunting shadows. A dead end waited for her with multiple boxes of empty bottles stacked up against the wall. She reached between the two middle boxes and pushed a stone button with a click that unveiled a secret passage behind her.

Emilia rolled her eyes. The whole cloak and dagger thing wasn't for her. She missed how easy it was to meet with people at a cafe for a drink or see a movie at the cinema. Instead, she was trapped in a place where she had to wear multiple masks every day to survive.

No. Thinking like that will get me nowhere.

Nothing would change anyway. She clenched her hands and marched in through the secret door. A dozen stone steps led her to a well-lit room with plenty of comfortable seating. An old desk, filled to the brim with parchments and letters, stood next to a huge iron safe at the back.

She looked around for Lionhart. Usually, he would be waiting for her with a warm drink at the ready. He was always early for his important guests and clients, which was why she liked him.

Emilia spotted a pair of muddy boots under the table. She made her way over and saw a mop of dark, curly hair splayed out over the remaining free space of the desk. The man in question was drooling on an unfinished letter.

How can he sleep with a bottle in hand and the smell of alcohol wafting from his body?

Then, realisation dawned on her. Today was the day Lionhart hated the most. Every year, his phantom leg pain flared up from whatever trauma he was trying to bury deep within his heart. So, he drank. A lot. He never explained the reason behind his false right leg or the long, thin scar on his neck.

She nudged his shoulder. "Would you like a drink of water to sober up?"

Lionhart groaned. "Go...way, E-sto!"

Emilia lowered her hood and made her way to the small table nearby on which a silver jug, filled with water, was perched next to two goblets.

She asked him for the last time, "Will you drink some water?"

He grunted loudly and swung his hand out in frustration. "Get out!"

"Very well." Taking the jug, she poured its contents over his head.

"What did you do tha—" His squinting eyes finally focused on her. "Oh, it's Her Majesty the Queen of this muck heap."

"I'm still Emilia to you, Lionhart, and it's not nice to call your guild names." She handed him the jug and sat on the cushioned chair, facing the mess she made with a smirk.

He ran a hand over his face and eyed the damage to his desk. "You could have spared the paperwork…"

"You never keep important documents out in the open. It was probably rumours so old that even the horses outside know about them."

Lionhart pushed his wet curls out of his brown eyes. His expression relaxed as he put on his professional smile. He wasn't a tall man compared to Prince Thessian, though Lionhart had at least three inches on Emilia, who was five-foot-four on a good day. He often wore baggy or unflattering clothes as if he had given up on attracting the opposite sex. If he had spared a moment to shave that awful shrub he called a beard and cut his hair enough to see his clients, he may not be bad-looking.

"Well, Emilia, what can I do for you this *wonderful* evening?"

Crossing her arms over her chest, she rebuked, "You could have declined a meeting with me!"

"Who in their right mind would deny the Queen?"

She pressed her lips into a tight line. Was he hung up on her new title? "I haven't changed overnight, Lionhart. I may be the Queen of Dante but more people want me dead than those who wish for me to live."

He pushed aside some of his drenched paperwork, causing some of the parchments to fall. Taking a seat on the edge of his desk, he used his hands for support at his sides. "You being among the living means it went well with Hellion's second prince."

"He doesn't trust me, and I am not foolish enough to give him my trust, either."

"Good. Trust is for those who can afford it. In your current situation, it is a hindrance."

Emilia folded her hands in her lap. Her fingers tightened their grip. "Did you get the evidence on the duke's family?"

He tilted his head towards the safe. "I got the reports and the witness's statements that Malette has been taking bribes and selling metal ores to the Reyniel Kingdom. His actions allowed them to manufacture a lot of military equipment that helped Reyniel in the past year with Dante's southern border. The Duchess has not kept her hands clean, either. Her invitation-only tea parties for nobility involved plenty of debaucheries and illegal drug abuse. She kept things quiet by blackmailing the nobles who wanted to leave." His eyes wrinkled with excitement. "I'm amazed a child like you came up with an idea of planting spies in the duke's home when you were barely thirteen. Now, you'll have enough evidence to have his family's heads rolling all the way to Reyniel."

She blushed. As this was her second life, she was mentally over forty, which was five years older than Lionhart.

"Ah, I went and embarrassed the Queen."

"I'll need a copy of the information to be delivered to the palace tomorrow. Give it to Sir Rowell."

"Not Ambrose? Are you testing the head butler?"

"He provides sound advice. I wish for more people like that to be on my side."

Lionhart crossed his arms over his chest. "What will you do if Sir Rowell doesn't pass on the documents to you? It would be a major blow to you when trying to convict Duke Malette."

Emilia didn't want to become a tyrant, yet she needed to clean house. Getting rid of anyone who may betray her in the future was the first logical step. "I will behead him and, of course, take back the originals with me today."

He nodded. "I thought so. I had Sally make copies this morning as you like your information to be supplied in triplicate."

She smiled. "I cannot thank you enough."

"You already have by making me one of the richest and busiest men in the kingdom."

She eyed his empty bottle on the desk. "Not busy enough."

"You know I hate it when people pry into my business."

Emilia gathered her courage as she formulated her response. He was going to deny her next request because he despised dealing with nobility. Yet, no matter what, she needed him at the palace. "Since you are so free, I would like for you to take on the role of my spymaster."

His expression darkened, and he got up. "I sincerely hope that was a terrible joke."

Rising from her seat, she lowered her head. "I understand this is a lot to ask. I will not ask you to attend events with the nobles. You could even use a stand-in for official meetings, but I need you by my side." She knew how weak she sounded. No queen would ever consider lowering their head to a man below their station, not to mention a commoner. "You have taught me how to fight, how to survive, and how to utilise the information in front of me. It would be foolish and arrogant of me to think that I can run this kingdom on my own."

"I am not qualified. Find someone else."

Her hands trembled at her sides. "Let's have a duel."

His eyes grew wide. "What?"

"If I win, you will become the spymaster."

He chuckled. "And when I win?"

"I won't bother you with this again."

"Although it is not much of a deal, I accept."

Emilia blew out a breath. She had sparred with Lionhart once a week in the past. He taught her how to use a dagger, a sword, and many defence techniques. Until now, she had never managed to win against her teacher. Even with a false leg, he moved quickly and crushed her defences with decisive manoeuvres.

Tonight, she had to win. Lionhart had to come to her side.

"I will call Sally to be the judge," he said on his way out of the room. He used the normal door that joined with the rest of the guild.

The inner courtyard was often used for training and sparring by the guild members. Emilia went on ahead.

Cold winter air bit her face when she arrived outside. The moon peeked out from behind gloomy clouds that sluggishly drifted across the starry sky. Oil lanterns illuminated the guild's inner courtyard, providing a comforting golden glow.

Ten minutes later, Lionhart emerged from the guild's hall with Sally in tow. She was a dwarf with a heart of gold.

One evening, after intense sparing with the guild master, Sally told Emilia about her past. When Sally's family was exiled from the Garhue Mountains, her father abandoned her roadside along with her human mother. Her mother worked in a brothel to pay for their new lives and passed away from an illness that covered her willowy body in sores. The rest of the symptoms sounded too much like syphilis to Emilia, but the doctors in Dante had yet to identify and name that disease.

After her mother's death, Sally could no longer stay there, she became a street rat who traded information for meals until Lionhart found her and took her in. At that time, the guild had yet to be formed. Lionhart taught Sally to read and write in multiple languages. That knowledge only solidified Emilia's belief that Lionhart used to be an important noble in another nation. Though, his skills in martial arts, fighting with weapons, and knowledge of the world indicated a different profession—one in which people did not live long or could leave with their life.

Sally came over to Emilia and greeted her with a warm smile. "Are you sure you want to do this? He won't go easy on you."

"I know." Emilia removed her cloak and handed it to Sally, who folded it neatly.

Lionhart tossed a shortsword in front of Emilia. As she picked it up, she noticed a small crowd had begun gathering to watch the show.

"Think it'll end like always?" one of the guild members muttered to another.

"'Course it will," came the chuckling reply.

Ernesto waltzed in, still dressed as a woman. He clapped his hands and grinned. "Someone, get the betting pool going! I'm going to bet on Lady Em."

Emilia glared at Lionhart. "You called them here on purpose!"

"Why? Do you think you'll have performance issues?"

Lionhart swung his shortsword in a practice swing to test its weight. He moved to stand three metres away from Emilia.

Raising his blade and pointing it at her, he asked, "Shall we begin?"

Emilia bit back a curse. She blocked out the chattering of the crowd that had already formed a loose circle around them. Sally was standing a safe distance away in the front row. The people in the guild showed Sally the same respect they showed Lionhart. After all, she managed the books and sorted through the information like none other.

"Remember what I taught you, Lady Em." Lionhart used her pseudonym in front of others. "There is no right or wrong in a fight."

Emilia clenched the hilt of the shortsword in her hand and nodded. She was as ready as she was going to get. After all, she had spent countless nights training alone in her tower's courtyard after each session with Lionhart. He was a great instructor and, fortunately, corrected many of her self-taught mistakes.

With Lionhart's speech over, he launched an attack. For his false leg to withstand real combat, he had paid quite a fortune. Despite his lean build, the impact of his swings felt like she was trying to block a sledgehammer with tin foil. Most of his attacks, she managed to dodge by jumping back or ducking at the last second. Not once was she able to initiate an attack, not to mention land a hit. She was completely on the defensive from the moment the duel began.

Does he hate the idea of being my spymaster that much?

Emilia felt his blade cutting into her arm in the moment of her distraction. Panting, she parried his move at the last second and kicked out, forcing him to back away. Ignoring the pain, an idea came to mind. It was dumb and dangerous. To win, she had to do it.

Lionhart narrowed his eyes when she changed her stance and launched at him. He easily deflected her attack and made a countermove, which she was hoping for. As his blade cut into her shoulder, she dropped her sword, caught it with her other hand and pressed the blade against his throat.

"I win!" Emilia spoke through gritted teeth.

Lionhart stared at her, dumbfounded. He pushed her sword away and shouted, "Are you insane?" His concern for her won over all other emotions.

The crowd had gone completely silent.

Lionhart told them to scatter, asking a select few to gather materials to treat her wound.

Sally handed him a wad of linen towels that he used to press against Emilia's bleeding wound. He picked her up as if she weighed nothing and carried her back to his office.

Emilia hissed in pain as she was lowered onto his cleared desk. His damp paperwork was scattered around the floor as if a tornado had flown in.

"Pour alcohol on the wound. I don't want to catch an infection," Emilia instructed.

Lionhart grumbled about how recklessly she acted and followed her advice by drenching her shoulder in his best bottle of mulberry gin. "We may need to cauterize the wound to stop the bleeding. It will leave a terrible scar. For a woman—"

She held on to his shirt's sleeve. "Do what must be done. I trust you."

"I am the last person you should be saying that to." His panic was enough for her to know that he cared about her in his own way. They had become good friends, and she hoped they could continue their partnership in the future. Hopefully, she would live long enough to find out the reason why he lost his leg and discarded his past.

"Lionhart," Emilia began in a strained voice, "you must bring me to my room before sunrise."

Sally and Ernesto rushed into the office with their hands full.

Everything thereafter was a blur. Emilia lost interest in the events around her. She was slowly growing light-headed, which didn't bode well. Blood transfusions weren't discovered yet. If she lost too much blood, no amount of human intervention would save her.

"Eat this for the pain." Sally gave Emilia a small ball-shaped pill that tasted so bitter, it was a struggle to swallow it.

After a short while, her drowsiness met with lightness in her limbs. Emilia felt like she was floating on air as Sally cut the material around Emilia's stab wound.

When Lionhart arrived with a heated knife in hand, Emilia didn't seem to care. It was only when the hot blade touched her exposed wound that the painkillers failed to do their duty.

Emilia's haze was replaced with burning agony. She clenched her teeth so hard; she thought her jaw would snap.

A scream tore through her.

Ernesto used this opportunity to stuff a gag in Emilia's mouth. "I'm sorry for this, Lady Em…"

Through tear-filled eyes, she moaned and felt her grasp on reality lessening. The pain was too much to handle. Emilia had underestimated the amount of torment she would be in. After all, the TV shows in the Modern Age made cauterisation seem like child's play.

God, this seriously hurts!

7
COLD-HEARTED PRINCE

LAURENCE

After escorting **Prince Thessian** to their hidden camp not far from Newburn, Laurence rode his horse back to the city. Everything from architecture to the people lacked life. He slowed his horse to a trot on a cobbled street.

How could the king let things deteriorate to such an extent? Was his greed worth this misery?

As a son of Marquess Oswald, he was taught to respect the people in his father's domain. There was no chance of him claiming that title for himself as he was the third son, and he was happy about it. He left the decision-making to the leader types. As a royal knight, it was his job to find the right master and serve them until death. Thessian was the person Laurence had chosen. Not because Thessian wanted the throne or wished to unite the continent.

The answer was much simpler.

Laurence enjoyed watching Thessian struggle to make conversation with the ladies at the balls or attending formal events where dancing was involved. In those moments, Laurence felt like he was of real use instead of acting as a shadow for some noble.

The other two princes of the Hellion Empire were proficient in small talk. Prince Cain turned heads wherever he went, as did his beautiful wife. Prince Kyros could talk all day about gossip and the happenings in the kingdom. He spent a mountain of gold to keep up to date with the latest fashion trends, though his physical shape often struggled to remain within the confines of the tailor's stitches.

Laurence tugged on the reins, making his horse come to a stop. Hopping off the saddle, he tied the reins to the nearest post and scanned the thinning crowd. The sun hid over the horizon, and most of the merchants were on their way home.

Instead of going to enjoy an ale with friends, Laurence was forced to query the local information guild. Thessian seemed determined to know whether Princess Emilia lied, which involved a lot of legwork. Due to their circumstances, Laurence could not use their messengers or the spymaster, who was related to Marquess Walden by blood. Their plans for Dante's coup were coming undone. Marquess Walden would be furious to find he was no longer required as regent or that Dante's only princess had claimed her authority without much effort.

Did she plan the whole thing?

Emilia was no simple girl who enjoyed painting and embroidery. She had sharp intellect reflected in her eyes that kept Laurence on guard. *How could a child come up with such a risky strategy, dig up information on the enemies, all the while being supposedly locked away in a tower...*

Is someone backing her? She didn't seem like a puppet.

He pulled on his hood and entered the tavern. The floorboards creaked under his weight as he made his way to an empty table at the back. His entrance was muffled by the drunken sputtering and chatter of the other patrons.

A busty barmaid glided over to his table with a cheerful smile. She resembled the barman, so Laurence assumed it was a family-owned business. "Would you like a drink or a meal, sir?"

Laurence lifted his head for her to see his face. He smiled brightly. "A meal and a drink would be wonderful, kind lady."

The girl, although plain in appearance, turned the colour of the Empire's scarlet flag. She fanned her face with her hand. "Oh my! I am a mere commoner, not a lady..."

He leaned closer to her. "In my eyes, you are as charming as any princess." Getting comfortable on the bench, he asked, "What would you recommend?"

She lowered her head as if to hide her embarrassment. "Our freshly-made meat pie and beer. I helped brew it myself."

When she lifted her eyes, Laurence winked. "I can't wait to taste it." Before she could scurry off, Laurence added, "I'm new to this city. Would you happen to know of any good information guilds?"

The girl replied almost immediately with a smile that made his day. "There is only one—the Lionhart Guild. You should be able to find it towards the back end of Market Street."

"Thank you kindly, my lady."

She bobbed her head and ran off.

Laurence rested his face on his fist as he observed the other patrons from under his hood. A few men stole glances his way. He doubted any of them were crooks or bandits. Most of the patrons were dressed better than mere commoners or miners and did not appear to be carrying anything bigger than a dagger. They were probably merchants or lower-class nobility.

The barmaid brought his meal a short while later. It tasted better than the military rations he had put up with since they left Darkgate. The other knights in his unit were going to be jealous. At least, Laurence had a place he could suggest to them. Thessian owed his men a hot meal after they got through the snowy Hollow Mountains and a coup.

He paid for his meal, leaving a tip for the service, and took his horse to search for the guild. Surprisingly, the guild was easy to spot. It was the only building on the street that had more than two storeys and took up three stores worth of space. They had to be making a lot of money, which was good for him. As long as the price was fair, he could entrust them with looking into the details of Marquess Walden and Thessian's spymaster.

He tied his horse in front of the guild and made his way inside. He was half-expecting limestone and marble decor but was met with simple wooden furniture and a bunch of burly men who were too busy playing cards to notice him.

At the back, Laurence spied a desk with a child who couldn't be older than ten. The boy was busy picking his ear with his pinkie, which made Laurence grimace.

Perhaps, they are the only guild because they extort others?

He pulled his hood farther over his face and proceeded to greet the boy.

On approach, the boy eyed Laurence with a piercing state. "Evenin', Sir Knight."

Laurence stilled mid-stride. How could the boy know he was a knight when Laurence did his best to imitate the walk of a mercenary? He also didn't wear any armour.

"Don't look so surprised." The boy crossed his arms over his small chest in an attempt to seem intimidating. "I've lived on dem streets long enough t'be able t'tell a noble from a rat an' a knight from a sellsword."

Laurence was at a loss for words. A child had cut through his disguise with a single look. "You are a very observant young man."

The boy jutted his chin out and proudly proclaimed, "Of course, I am!" His eyes widened when he saw a dwarf coming into the guild's hall. "Drat! Sally's 'ere. I'm dead if she finds me." He waved to Laurence and ducked down under the desk.

From where Laurence stood, he could see the young boy crawling away on all fours to not catch the attention of that woman.

Sally noticed Laurence standing at the desk. She hurried over, shooting disapproving looks at the gambling men. "Greetings, milord. Are you here on business?"

"I am here to buy some information." It was the first time Laurence had seen such a delicate woman. He heard a handful of crude tales about the dwarves during small talk with the nobles and knew how humans treated them. "Could you tell me where the guild master is? The matter I want to discuss is quite important."

Sally wrinkled her face. "Today is not a good day to meet him…"

"Is he busy?" Laurence doubted that, as most of the guild members were occupied with gambling in the open. The guild master had to be in an equally eventful situation.

"He is feeling under the weather, milord."

"Sally!" A man burst in with a slight limp to his gait. He looked as if he had barely gotten out of his bout of drinking.

Laurence's eyes widened when he noted the man's dark skin as it was considered exotic on the continent.

"What are you doing, running around looking like that?" Sally scolded the man twice her size while she rested her hands on her hips.

Scratching his mop of unruly curls, the man spoke loud enough for the others to easily overhear. "Lady Em and I are going to have a duel. You must be the judge."

The young boy from earlier peeked out from behind the man's back. His round eyes sparkled with excitement. "A duel? It's been a while." He started to shout, "Oi, freeloaders! Lionhart is 'bout t'duel!"

By the time Laurence realised that the strange man was the guild master, Lionhart and Sally were gone. Scanning the room, he saw the men scrambling for one of the doors, abandoning their cards and chips on the tables.

Laurence sighed heavily. "What kind of guild is this? Everyone must have lost their minds." Well, he may as well enjoy a fight before tracking Lionhart down for information. He followed the others to a large enclosed courtyard where a betting game was happening among the guild members.

The crowd had surrounded two people in the middle.

He got closer for a better view, and his jaw fell open. He couldn't believe his eyes. Partaking in the duel, with a shortsword in hand, was the Queen of Dante. He rubbed his eyes and took another look.

No, I'm not seeing things…

Laurence reached for his sword to stop them but felt heavy hands on his sword arm and both shoulders.

To his right, an older man with a scarred face spoke in a gruff voice. "Ya better not interfere."

Laurence ground his teeth. There were, at least, five men keeping an eye on him. All of them had a sword strapped to their hips. As he withdrew his hand from the hilt of his sword, he watched the fight unfolding with utter disbelief. Princess Emilia, despite living in a tower her entire life, defended herself as well as any seasoned knight would. With a bit more training, she could put up a fight against Cali, whom Laurence had spent four years instructing.

Lionhart was not going easy on her. He left no openings for her to strike after she managed to deflect or dodge his attacks. The duel's outcome was obvious.

As if Emilia had not surprised Laurence enough in the past two days, she did so once more when she purposefully let Lionhart's sword pierce her shoulder. On impulse, Laurence wanted to run to her side and inched forwards.

Once again, he was prevented by the same scarred onlooker.

The crowd's nervous chatter was interrupted by Lionhart ordering the others to scatter.

"Time to go," the scarred man muttered and pushed Laurence back to the guild's hall.

Reluctantly, he went along with the guild members. Dread filled his stomach. That was no simple wound. Emilia could be dead before dawn. What was going through her head to act so recklessly?

Does she have a death wish? Then why did she bargain with Prince Thessian?

He was offered a seat at one of the tables and given a goblet of cheap ale that was on par with ditch water. The scarred man and the boy from earlier sat across from Laurence on a wooden bench.

The boy spoke first. "What's your name, Sir Knight?"

"Laurel." Laurence used his pseudonym outside of Hellion. He wasn't about to share his real name with them in case the guild members knew of Prince Thessian's close aides. "And you are?"

"I'm Rime," the boy replied and pointed to the scarred man. "He's Jehan."

"Do ya know Lady Em?" Jehan asked.

Laurence shook his head. "Not well. I only met her once." Which wasn't a lie. "Does she come here often?"

"Lady Em is Lionhart's sweet'art!" Rime claimed.

Jehan elbowed the boy in the ribs. "Stop babbling."

Laurence clenched his fists. "Shouldn't you be more concerned about her? She got seriously injured."

Jehan gave a curt nod. "She did, but she trusted the guild master to take care of her. He won't let her die."

"Right! It's 'cause they're secret L-A-V-E-R-Z."

Slapping the back of Rime's head, Jehan grumbled, "Secret lovers don't go about duelling each other. They must be just friends."

"You've been single for ages 'cause o' that face o' yours," Rime countered, smiling knowingly. "What would you know?" He directed his attention to Laurence. "Laurel's got a portrait-pretty mug. I'm sure ladies flock t'him from dusk till dawn."

Laurence raised his hands in defence. "I assure you, I am not that popular."

Rime snorted. "Right…"

The conversation was getting Laurence nowhere. Although he came there for information on Marquess Walden, there was no way for him to get it now. He had to report what happened to His Highness.

Would Prince Thessian even care? He does not know Emilia well.

Laurence finished his drink and got up from the table. "I will return tomorrow."

"Leavin' already?" Rime appeared deflated.

"There are duties I must attend to." Laurence excused himself and left the guild empty-handed.

His mind raced with the thoughts of what they would do if Emilia died at the hands of the guild master. Lifting his gaze briefly to the sky, he mumbled a quick prayer for her as well as made a mental note to scold Cali for failing in her duties.

By the time Laurence returned to camp, it was the middle of the night. Most of the knights were sleeping on their bedrolls. Laurence made sure to check in with the knights on guard duty, then went to Thessian's tent.

No one was there.

Laurence followed the grunting coming from the other side of the treeline, near a small creek. His heavy steps revealed his presence to the prince before he had a chance to get too close.

"You have returned." Thessian continued to swing his sword.

Laurence rubbed the back of his neck. He wasn't certain how much of that night's events he needed to reveal to the prince. Instead, he opted to lighten the mood first. "I have been rushed off my feet all day. I even skipped dinner to search for the information guild."

Thessian stopped and faced Laurence. "You look too spirited to have skipped a meal."

"Alright, you caught me." Laurence patted his stomach. "I ate in a tavern. You should bring the others there for a meal. The food is decent."

"What about the task I gave you?"

"I didn't get far. I may need some time to get you answers, Your Highness."

Thessian resumed his training, which meant Laurence was dismissed.

Laurence's curiosity wouldn't let him leave. He wanted to know how much the news of Emilia's duel would affect the prince. Thessian had never openly shown interest in the opposite sex. At least, not since his first love got married while he was away at war. It had been eight years since then.

When will he move on?

Laurence was growing tired of correcting the nobles who

suspected His Highness wasn't interested in women and preferred the company of men.

"I did see something interesting..." Laurence began as he shoved his hands into his pockets to keep them warm. "Emilia left the castle for a sword fight."

The prince's swing faltered. "Are you certain it was her?"

"Last I checked, I have good eyesight."

"I see."

Laurence raised a brow. *What a boring response...*

In a way, Laurence hoped Prince Thessian would drop everything, mount his horse, and rush off to the palace. But that was a fantasy perfect for romance novels the ladies of the court enjoyed reading in private. Unlike in Laurence's made-up tale, Thessian resumed his practice as if nothing happened.

On his way back to the campsite, Laurence called over his shoulder, "Oh, and she got severely hurt."

It could have been Laurence's imagination, but he was almost certain he heard Thessian cursing under his breath.

8
STRANGE HOBBIES

EMILIA

Emilia would have sold her crown for an effective pain relief that did not require her being unconscious for a day or a mage with a strong healing ability. Maybe, instead of avoiding the hero of the novel as she had originally planned, she could seduce him and keep him by her side as a personal first aid kit. The problem was that he wasn't going to awaken his magic until after Prince Thessian's death. Magic was a complicated subject. The Royal Library had a limited number of books about the subject because the previous king paid it no mind. Hiring a mage to serve in court would cost a fortune for some party tricks. Other than showing off in front of other royals, there was no point in it. Not like the mages could tear the sky apart or bring someone back from the dead.

"How are you feeling?" Lionhart, who was supporting most of her weight, asked.

Is he serious?

Emilia sluggishly turned her head to see his face. She couldn't tell if he was joking or not in the darkness of the castle's catacombs.

"I shouldn't have asked…" he mumbled.

In front of them, Ernesto held an oil lantern high, still donned in his gown and casting a wide silhouette.

"We are almost there. Another right turn here," Emilia instructed.

At last, they managed to get to the secret passage to her bedchambers. She thought she would faint halfway there. The herbal painkillers or whatever it was Sally had fed her, were only able to suppress some of the suffering. Every time Emilia moved her arm or shoulder, a jolt of excruciating pain shot through her body, and she saw stars.

Did I make a mistake? Will I die from an infection because I don't have any antibiotics around? I should have studied pharmacology in my previous life.

Emilia pushed the unlocking mechanism in the shape of a star, making the stone wall slide open for them.

Ernesto and Lionhart helped her into the bedroom.

She was ready to collapse when she saw a proud Ambrose sitting on top of an assassin. From head to toe, he was completely subdued with expertly made knots. Emilia wasn't the only one at a loss for words. The way that poor assassin was tied up, with a rag stuffed into his mouth, looked like a scene out of a bondage play.

Surely, Ambrose isn't into that kind of thing…

"Your Majesty, you have returned!" Ambrose jumped up full of excitement until she took a look at the blood on Emilia's clothes. She rushed over, white as a sheet. "Who did this to you?"

Emilia laughed it off. "I got into a small fight."

Ernesto peered past Ambrose's head. "What did you do to him?"

"Her Majesty told me to capture the assassin," the maid replied.

"Did you have to tie him up like that?" Ernesto gave the unconscious man a pitying look. "That seems…excessive."

Ambrose shrugged. "I had to make sure he would not take his

life."

Emilia decided it was time to change the topic. Ambrose used to work at the docks when she was staying at the orphanage. *She must have picked up her rope-tying skills there*, Emilia concluded. "I am glad you were able to fend him off."

As Ambrose was about to reply, the door to her room burst open. In the doorway stood Prince Thessian, wearing a mixture of concern and anger on his face. Emilia nearly fell backwards from the levels of intimidation that rolled off him.

Lionhart inched to stand in front of her, obviously trying to protect her from the rude intruder.

Emilia gave the guild master's arm a light squeeze and pushed away from him. The sharp movement hurt so much; she was ready to burst into tears on the spot. Through pure perseverance, she managed to keep her expression mostly neutral. "Your Highness, it is awfully rude to invade a lady's bedchambers at such a late hour. Don't you think?"

Thessian blinked in utter confusion. He looked from Emilia to her friends to the tied-up assassin. "Is slight impropriety on my part what we should concern ourselves with here?" He narrowed his sharp gaze on Lionhart who, at some point, managed to get his shortsword out without Emilia noticing. Ignoring the visible threat, he said, "I heard you got hurt."

Emilia wanted to slap herself. How did the prince, of all people, find out about her duel before anyone else? She glared at Lionhart who shook his head apologetically. It couldn't have been his guild members. They may be a rowdy bunch, but they would never betray the guild and leak what happened within its walls.

So, who was it?

Emilia's head began to spin. She reached out, and Ambrose caught her by the elbow. "Ambrose, get the royal physician. Tell him to wait outside until I say so."

Ambrose helped Emilia to her bed and walked out of the room as fast as was permissible in front of royalty.

"What should we do about him?" Lionhart pointed to the assassin.

Emilia raised her voice. "Dame Cali?"

The knight opened the door and strode inside. For some reason, Cali seemed dejected. It didn't take long for Emilia to guess why. Behind her, in the doorway, was Sir Laurence.

"You called, Your Majesty?" Cali asked with a formal bow.

"Please escort that man to the dungeon and ask trustworthy men from Prince Thessian's unit to guard him. He cannot escape or die under any circumstances."

Cali made a nervous glance in Thessian's direction.

The prince merely nodded, and Cali followed the order.

Sitting on the bed put less strain on Emilia but did nought to silence the ringing in her ears.

Am I suffering from too much blood loss?

She hoped the physician wasn't going to give her any bad news. As far as she had read, the medicine of Dante's Kingdom revolved around bloodletting and leeches. She didn't want to partake in either. Would it have killed her father to invest in medical research?

"You should lie down," Lionhart suggested. "Your complexion is on par with the marble fireplace."

That coaxed a smile out of Emilia.

Ernesto helped her climb under the covers while Prince Thessian glared daggers at Lionhart.

"As you can see, Your Highness, I am perfectly fine. You needn't worry about me," Emilia assured Thessian.

Thessian raised a brow. "There is enough blood on your clothes to say otherwise."

Lionhart seemed to agree. "You were too reckless today."

Everyone was treating her like she was some child who didn't know what she was doing. Granted, she didn't anticipate the extent of the damage she would take. Yet, she managed to win the duel and get enough evidence to put Duke Malette on trial for treason.

"After the king died, I thought I would be without a father. Now, it seems, I have two."

Ernesto stifled a laugh while Thessian and Lionhart appeared like they were ready to vomit blood. Though, looking closely, Lionhart seemed unhappy for a different reason than Prince

Thessian. He never told Emilia about his family. She knew next to nothing about him from the novel because he was a side character Thessian met with briefly. Lionhart held too many secrets, and she sensed that prying them open would cause their fragile friendship to crumble. Seeing the two of them in the same room was good for her heart. She wondered how they would react if she told them that in another world, they had fans who often drew them in a passionate embrace. Lionhart and Thessian would sail the seven seas together if the fandom had their way.

"Are you plotting dangerous things again?" Lionhart asked her with suspicion.

Was I being too obvious? "Not at all..."

"I am only twenty-seven," Thessian muttered as if his brain finally finished processing her words.

Lionhart grumbled under his breath. He reached into the inner pocket of his coat and pulled out a thick stack of papers. "Where do you want me to leave these, *Your Majesty*?"

She grimaced at the forced way he used her title in front of Thessian. "Leave them with Ambrose."

Lionhart bowed. "With your permission, I will take my leave."

"Don't forget to keep your word," she reminded him.

"As you know, my word is my bond. I must make some arrangements and will join you when ready."

Emilia was pleased. She wouldn't need to sneak out of the palace for a while with him there. "Thank you."

On his way out with Ernesto, Lionhart seemed cautious around Prince Thessian. He muttered a half-baked greeting and left.

"Are you not leaving, Your Highness?" Emilia wanted things to settle, so she could rest. Why couldn't the men in her life understand that? Then again, Thessian had no reason to care about her well-being. He only spared her because she got him curious about a possible betrayal of Marquess Walden.

He got closer and loomed over her. Reading his expression proved difficult when his dark green eyes seemed to drill into her. "What are you planning?"

"Everything I do is for you, Your Highness."

Doubt was evident on his face. "Why would you do that? I killed your family and almost killed you." He ran his hand through his messy blond hair. "Why did you stay in the tower when you could have escaped? Why bother helping me? What are you planning?"

He had enough questions to last the remainder of the night. Emilia would pass out at any moment. Her body was barely able to stay alert from the stress and shock it underwent. "I promise to answer every one of your questions if you would return for tea once I am feeling better." She knew he wouldn't be satisfied with that alone. "Soon, I plan on dismantling the hold Duke Malette has on the nobility and removing any nobles who support him." Emilia bowed her head slightly but kept their eyes locked, which pulled on the muscles in her wounded shoulder. She winced. "I will serve you, Your Highness, to the best of my ability."

"You are a strange young lady." Thessian stepped back from her bedside. "Get some rest. I will return once I verify the information you have given me."

"Thank you for giving me a chance."

He headed out without a reply, which she took as an acknowledgement that she could proceed with her plans.

Ambrose called from the other side of the door, "Your Majesty, the royal physician is here."

"Let him in."

The person behind Ambrose was a hunched-over man in his late fifties. He must have been woken from his sleep as he was wearing his white nightshirt under a light-grey cloak.

The physician spotted the blood on Emilia's clothing. He bowed low and asked in a nervous tone, "Your Majesty, I am Benjamin Baudelaire. May I examine your wound?"

Emilia mentally noted that he had to be related to Count Baudelaire. "You may."

With steady hands, Benjamin thoroughly examined her sealed wound and her vital signs. "May I ask what happened?"

"An assassin came into my room and attacked me. That is all you need to know."

He nodded. "It would seem you have lost a lot of blood, Your

Majesty. Any work that needs to be done must be postponed for at least two weeks. I will prepare a salve to put on your wound to ease the pain and help reduce the scarring." He hung his head. "My knowledge is not enough to prevent scarring entirely, Your Majesty. I am truly sorry for my incompetence."

Emilia didn't care, yet every person so far treated the scar as if it was a huge deal. Sure, it would be hard to find a man who appreciated a woman with a damaged body as most noblewomen put in tremendous effort to look like picture-perfect statues. It's not like she couldn't find a husband. She was a queen. Her status alone would bring her some suitors. Not as many, but some. She clenched her fist. She wasn't planning on marriage anyway. Her goal was to get Thessian indebted to her and live off her investments. In the meantime, if she could fix a few problems in Dante, that would be a bonus for her conscience.

"I am rather tired. Bring me my medicine, so I can rest." She narrowed her eyes on the doctor. "Make sure to keep this to yourself."

"Understood." He excused himself and backed out of the room.

Ambrose pouted. "Your Majesty, you must change your clothes before you sleep."

Emilia glanced at her bloodstained tunic and undershirt. "Very well. Once we finish, call for Sir Rowell."

"He is waiting for your orders outside," Ambrose replied as she rummaged through the armoire.

Sir Rowell was good at his job. He must have noticed the commotion and knew he would be needed.

Once the physician had finished his treatment, Emilia looked like a mummy from her chest to her neck. Thankfully, her night dress covered most of the bandages.

"Invite Sir Rowell in," Emilia instructed.

The maid summoned the head butler who arrived promptly.

Sir Rowell didn't ask any unnecessary questions or pry into her state of well-being. He must have already asked everyone around them. "Your orders, Your Majesty?"

"Have the Captain of the Guard watch Duke Malette and

anyone who entered the palace with him. They cannot leave the palace grounds until my say so."

The butler had an apologetic look on his face. "Your Majesty, the captain was killed protecting King Gilebert."

"Oh." *Damn.* She needed to appoint a new captain, too. "Tell Dame Cali Louberte to fill the role until I find a suitable replacement."

"Is there anything else you need?"

Emilia could tell him that important papers were due to arrive tomorrow but thought better of it. She needed to test him and tipping him off that she was expecting documents from the guild would defy the point. "Have a written confession from the assassin secured no matter what while I rest."

"Yes, Your Majesty." Sir Rowell followed royal protocol and made his exit.

"Please get some rest, Your Majesty," Ambrose suggested, standing in the corner of the room. "I will stay and keep watch."

Making Ambrose stay up all night would be too cruel. Somehow, Emilia knew that asking her maid to get some sleep would be met with resistance, so, instead, she said, "Don't stand there like a pillar. Take a seat on the chair. It will make me feel more comfortable."

Ambrose smiled. "Thank you for your kindness."

9
RESTRICTIONS

THESSIAN

There were few people in the world that Thessian could not figure out.

The first was his father, who refused to pick the crown prince and continuously tested his sons' devotion to Hellion. The second was his younger brother, Kyros. He always acted like he did not care for the crown and only wished to enrich himself via vile means. *Why would he go out of his way to bribe Marquess Walden who had been loyal to the emperor for decades?* Was it a lie on Emilia's part or an elaborate plot by the Marquess? Lastly, the person he understood the least was Emilia Dante.

No matter how he looked at it, she was unpredictable. She thought so far in advance that his head spun. How could a young lady like her scheme and plot the downfall of her family while putting herself in obvious danger for a foolish gamble?

Is it foolish?

Thessian knew he could not trust Emilia, but her eyes were clear and reflected honesty. She never once averted her gaze during their discussions or allowed for subconscious signs of deceit to surface.

Why would she want to make me emperor?

He raked his fingers through his hair in frustration as he headed to his horse at the stables.

Laurence caught up with him. "I did not think you would race down to see her, Your Highness. Is she your type?"

Thessian glared at his friend. "How could I be interested in a child? She got hurt while fulfilling her duty as my regent. I simply did not wish to look for another."

With a knowing smile, Laurence replied, "There is nothing wrong with admitting you care a bit about the Cursed Princess."

"Do not use that foul name." He hated when the nobles called him the 'Bloodthirsty Demon' since his return from the battlefield. Emilia most likely disliked that dreadful moniker. "I want you to bring my healing salve to her."

"You mean the one imbued with magic for the sole use of the Hellion Imperial Family?"

"Yes."

"The same one that costs one hundred gold for a single jar?"

"Yes, Laurence!" Thessian snapped.

Laurence snickered. "How fatherly of you."

Thessian tried to casually smack Laurence's head, but his friend avoided his hand.

"Calm yourself, Your Highness. It was but a jest. However, you should consider giving up your affections for the princess. She thinks you are old enough to be her father." Laurence spoke the last words between fits of laughter.

Thessian clenched his jaw and reminded himself that killing subordinates was bad for his image. "During morning training, I expect you to put in an extra hour."

Laurence's glee waned. "What? I was not serious. Please be merciful to this impertinent subject!"

Thessian reached the stables where he mounted his horse to the sound of Laurence's incessant pleas. "Make sure to run an extra ten miles."

"Your Highness, I am a man, not a horse."

"Perhaps, you should take some cues from this animal and talk less." Thessian nudged his horse with his heels and galloped back to their campsite.

10

UPHEAVAL

EMILIA

"**Your Majesty, please wake up,**" Ambrose's voice shattered Emilia's wonderful dream of a passionate kiss shared between Lionhart and Thessian.

Emilia wrinkled her brow as the pleasant image faded. Bright sunlight shone on her face, and she peeled her heavy eyelids apart. With wakefulness came the reminder of how much pain she was in. Even the smallest muscles in her body were complaining.

Sitting up without her maid's help was impossible. Her surviving the previous night had to be due to adrenaline. As a patient, she felt like she had been beaten up, put through a grinder, and then hit by a bus. She dreaded the events that awaited her later.

"Should I summon the physician to check on you?" Ambrose knotted her hands in front of her. She often did that when she was nervous.

Emilia probably looked terrible for Ambrose to be completely unable to conceal her emotions. "Go ahead."

Ambrose ran out faster than a hawk catching its prey.

Emilia heard a rap on the door.

From the other side, Sir Rowell announced himself. Tired of the endless formalities, Emilia urged him to come in. She wished for fewer rules and regulations on how people had to act around her but maintaining the royal image was equally as important. She was in a fragile situation as a new monarch and had to undergo a formal coronation which meant dealing with the Church of the Holy Light. That religion was full of strange myths and pointless superstitions. An archbishop of that blasted church was the one who prophesied on the day of her birth that she would bring about the downfall of the Dante Kingdom. Because of that idiotic prediction, she was treated like an outcast and kept in a cold tower for almost eighteen years. The thought of getting involved with those stuck-up priests, who sat on mounds of gold, gave her a bitter taste in her mouth.

By the time Emilia came out of her reverie, she realised she had made Sir Rowell wait. "Do you have any news on the assassin?"

"Yes, Your Majesty. After much persuasion, he admitted he was hired by the duke."

"Great. Have the guards seize Malette." She pursed her lips. She couldn't stop there. A purge was needed, or she could be in danger again. As much as she hated shedding blood, every king in the history of Dante had removed their enemies first after taking the throne. She couldn't act like a sheep in a lion's den. "Make sure to ask Dame Cali to keep an eye on his associates who entered the city."

"Yes, Your Majesty." Sir Rowell smiled at her kindly. "While I carry out your order, would you like your breakfast served here or in the dining hall?"

Emilia smiled back. "Here is fine. Thank you, Sir Rowell."

"It is my pleasure to serve Her Majesty."

The rest of her morning was uneventful. Emilia had her bandages changed and an herbal paste that smelled of burdock, thyme, and ginger was applied to her wound. With Ambrose's help, she took a much-needed bath and got dressed.

The physician stubbornly told Emilia not to move her arm until her injury healed, so she wound up having to tie it up. She looked ridiculous as a monarch, though no one dared comment within her earshot.

In the afternoon, while she was having tea in her office, Sir Rowell arrived with the documents from the guild. Emilia could finally breathe now that she knew the head butler was on her side.

Not long after, Cali asked for an audience.

"Your Majesty, I do not believe I am suitable for the position you have granted me."

Yes, it would be hard for you to spy on me while you are busy maintaining order in the castle. "Why would that be? You are an elite knight from Prince Thessian's army. I trust you will do well, and this assignment is only temporary."

"It is not a matter of ability. I am a foreigner, Your Majesty, and the men of Dante will not listen to me."

"I cannot tell them to listen to you. Look to your superiors for inspiration and use that to earn the respect of those men."

She seemed thoughtful for a minute. "You may be right. This could be an opportunity for me to understand Sir Laurence better."

Emilia cracked into a smirk. "Just Sir Laurence?"

"And Prince Thessian, of course!"

"Of course."

Cali's face and ears reddened. Emilia had to stop teasing her as she wanted Cali on her side.

Clearing her throat, Cali said, "We've received a report that Duke Malette may be assembling a private army in his territory. What would you have me do?"

War and strategy weren't Emilia's forte. She needed someone with experience, and she knew the perfect men for the job. "Could you invite Prince Thessian and Sir Laurence to the castle this evening? I wish to seek their advice."

Cali's expression brightened at the mention of Laurence. She was so obvious.

How on earth did he not notice it?

Was he pretending to be blind to avoid a relationship with someone under his command? Raking her mind for any slivers of information, Emilia couldn't recall a single scene in the novel where Laurence got together with Cali. Thessian avoided love and relationships, so he never cared to notice. With Thessian by Emilia's side, she didn't need to worry about him running off with some noblewoman and abandoning the throne or fearing that he might fall for her. They made perfect partners, neither interested in courtship nor marriage. One day, he would need to marry a princess to make a political alliance. He couldn't be selfish.

The day dragged on. Emilia had more than enough paperwork to sign for the funeral procession. The king would soon be buried six feet under, and she would get her chance to spit on that bastard's grave. Her brothers didn't even deserve a burial, in her opinion. They made her life miserable. To appear like she was grieving to the lords and the common folk, she had to put on a show, at least, for one day.

She had put off dinner until Thessian's and Laurence's arrival. Once they were seated at the table in the dining hall, she said, "Thank you for coming, Your Highness, Sir Laurence."

"It is a pleasure." Laurence grinned. "I finally get to eat a proper meal."

Thessian covered his eyes with his hand. "Ignore my subordinate, Your Majesty."

Emilia couldn't hold back a smile. Those two got along so well, she was getting jealous of their bond. "I don't mind. Sir Laurence is a breath of fresh air within these stuffy walls."

Laurence lifted his goblet of wine. "You are making me blush, Your Majesty. Had I been the one assigned as your guard, I would have been so much happier as I would get to see the most beautiful sight in the whole kingdom on a daily basis."

Flattery didn't work on Emilia. Out of politeness, she gave a mild nod. "Speaking of Dame Cali, did she fill you in on why I asked for this meeting?"

Thessian gave Laurence a warning glare. "The Duke is trying to gather forces."

"I am not well versed in military strategy," she admitted. Reading books on history and battles was one thing, but understanding the reasoning of the commanders in those accounts was another. Emilia was at a complete loss. It was easier to make money than staking the lives of thousands of men on a single battlefield. "I would appreciate any help you could offer, Your Highness."

The prince studied her face intently. He seemed like he stopped himself from saying what was on his mind. "We should eat first."

"Yes, you are right." Emilia forgot they were her guests and not simple advisors. With so much work piling up, she didn't feel hungry. Cutting into the boar meat with one hand also did not appeal to her.

"Bring in the food," she ordered the servants.

During their meal, Laurence filled most of the conversation with embellished tales of Thessian's heroic feats. There was no point in Sir Laurence's attempt to portray Thessian in a positive light to Emilia. She knew he was a strong leader and a caring friend from the original story. If anything, she was lucky to be seated across from him instead of being buried with her family.

Emilia patiently waited until Thessian finished his meal. "Did you enjoy your food, Your Highness?"

"I did. Thank you kindly for inviting us."

Laurence wiped his hands on the napkin. "It was delicious, Your Majesty."

"I will have your compliments passed on to the chef." She knotted her fingers in her lap. "Can we talk about the issue with the Duke's army?"

Thessian crossed his arms as he relaxed in his seat. "You have him in custody, do you not?"

"He is being kept under strict watch in the dungeon."

"Without him and his money, the Duke's army will fall apart. The problem will take care of itself as long as you manage to get rid of the man as soon as possible."

Emilia had to wait until after the king's funeral to deal with Malette's trial. There was no doubt in her mind he had spies in her palace. She could only rely on a select few.

Laurence added, "Malette could have arrangements with other nobles to pay for the military support. As long as the soldiers are being paid, they will not desert their posts."

"What does that mean exactly?" she asked, her nails digging into her palms.

Thessian elaborated, "We could have a civil war on our hands if the rebellion is not squashed in its first stages."

"But the king's loyal knights were killed in the coup, and I have no military force to call my own." Emilia shuddered at the possibility of having to deal with an uprising right after she got her hands on the throne. "Currently, the only people guarding the palace are those provided by you and Count Baudelaire."

Thessian's lips parted into a reassuring smile. "Believe me, I will do what I can to protect my new territory."

She blew out a sigh of relief. Thessian was a great commander and had spent many years on the battlefield. "I am glad to hear that."

"Laurence, leave us. I would like to discuss something with the Queen in private."

The knight wordlessly bobbed his head and strode out of the room.

Emilia dismissed the servants once they had tidied the table.

"Would you care for a stroll in the garden?" Thessian asked, getting up.

Not like she had a choice. Emilia promised to answer his questions the next time they met. Escaping wasn't an option.

"It would be my pleasure." She bit her lip. "I may require your support as I am quite tired after fulfilling my duties today."

He offered her his arm through which she slipped her hand. On the way to the garden, Ambrose provided Emilia with a warm cloak and gloves.

As the moon came out from behind the clouds that drifted across the blackening sky, its light illuminated the carefully manicured gardens ahead of them. King Gilebert had become a vanity fanatic in the past five years. He had some of the tall shrubs shaped to look like knights, fair maidens, and arches. By the fountain at the back of the lantern-lit maze, Gilebert placed a life-sized bronze statue of himself standing atop a pedestal. The unsightly work of art towered above the rest of the scenery and could be seen from almost everywhere in the garden.

When Emilia came to stand before it, she cringed.

"You did not like the king?" Thessian asked nonchalantly.

"King Gilebert was not a good father. He was more of an existence that made my life miserable while my brothers pushed it closer to unbearable."

He remained quiet as they strolled down the lit paths. The cool winter breeze made Emilia's cheeks and ears sting. She peeked at the prince, wondering if he was equally as uncomfortable.

"You had a lot of questions for me last night..." she began.

"I did. I mean, I do." Thessian stopped in front of a stone bench. "Please, take a seat."

Once she did, he joined her. The prince completely dismissed any formalities between them when they were alone. He was either extremely comfortable around her or did not see her as important enough to follow royal protocol. She leaned towards the latter.

"How did you know I was planning to invade Dante?" His scrutinizing stare made her uncomfortable in her skin. "We were in the early planning stages. Only those closest to me knew of it."

Emilia thought hard about an answer that would satisfy him. She couldn't exactly tell him she once read his entire life's story in a novel and was acting accordingly. He may even think she had lost her sanity in that tower and wasn't worth his investment or time.

"What about Marquess Walden? How did you know it was him I planned to use as regent? Only Laurence and the Marquess knew this."

I didn't think he would ask that...

His weariness and frustration rose above his gentlemanly mask. None too gently, he grabbed her wrist. "Are you, perhaps, able to *See*?"

Emilia's eyes widened. He was talking about the magical ability of foresight. Throughout the history of the continent, only two people possessed such a dangerous power. The first mage was treated like a God and given riches beyond his wildest dreams in return for his prophecies. In contrast, the second mage, who was born two hundred years later, was fought over by greedy kings who wished to use her. A sea of blood was spilt and many kingdoms fell as a consequence. The mage vanished for nearly a decade before she returned as the 'Saint of the Holy Light' and was used to increase the church's power. Because of that, their influence spanned the entire continent and infiltrated even the smallest of towns. Not long after, that mage was assassinated—a morbid tale.

Emilia couldn't keep silent. Thessian wanted answers, and the truth was more ridiculous than the idea of her having mythical powers.

"I...I don't know." Emilia lowered her head. "Sometimes, I happen to know when certain events will happen. It is not something I can control." She didn't want him to think she had the power of foresight at her beck and call.

The prince was silent for such a long time that she looked up.

Thessian appeared deep in thought. He ran his hand through his hair. "I can understand why you would keep your ability from others."

"Will you try to use me because of it, Your Highness?" If he wanted her non-existent ability, she would get Lionhart to ship her off to some no-name town where she could live out her life as a lonely spinster.

"Such a power could be of great benefit in becoming the Crown Prince of the Empire."

Emilia swallowed nervously. She already started planning how much gold she was going to take on her one-way trip and was in the middle of deciding whether to take Ambrose.

"I would not dream of forcing you. You have my word."

"Will you keep it a secret?"

He placed his hand over his heart, and their eyes met. "I, Prince Thessian Alexey Hellios, Duke of Darkgate, will take your secret to the grave should you wish it, my lady."

Emilia broke into tears as relief bubbled up in her stuffy chest.

She could stay in the palace a while longer and even found out his middle name which was never mentioned in the novel.

"I am glad I made the right choice." She wiped at her wet cheeks with her gloved hand.

"About what?"

"About choosing to support you."

Thessian quirked a brow and then shook his head. "I should not ask what future you saw."

"I will give you a hint." Her breath turned to steam in the cold. She distantly looked at the fountain in which the water had almost frozen from the temperature dropping for the night. "You should be wary of the third prince."

"I do not understand."

Her rear was getting chilled from the stone bench, so she got up and wrapped the cloak tighter around her with one hand. "You will in due time." She glanced back towards the palace. A nice hot bath would be perfect after the day she had. "We should be getting back."

He rose to his full height. "Of course. You should rest. Your wound must be hurting. I had Laurence bring something that will help with the scarring. He should have given it to your maid by now."

Emilia's cheeks warmed. He cared enough to give her a gift. All of his fangirls must be so jealous of her. "Thank you for your generosity, Your Highness. Your kindness is too much for someone like me."

"Pardon my rudeness." He gently touched her shoulder, which made her notice how big his hands were. "You underestimate your value a great deal. Please refrain from speaking like that again."

"I will try my best."

That night, she vowed to find him a gorgeous and kind princess that would match him once he ascended the throne. He deserved a happily ever after unlike the tyrannical third prince.

11
NOT ACCORDING TO PLAN

LAURENCE

Laurence tailed Prince Thessian and Queen Emilia throughout their stroll. Although the Queen was injured, he did not trust her. So far, she had acted unlike a noble lady. What was her goal? Did she want a crown? Or was she interested in securing marriage with Prince Thessian to remain in power?

When he overheard what was spoken between them, his stomach dropped.

She has the ability to See?

An ability that was sought after was right there, yet His Highness vowed not to share her secret or use her. Laurence slapped his forehead. Thessian was too kind for his own good. Why not use her ability to their advantage? It could easily make the Emperor of Hellion grant Thessian the position of the crown prince. She could be useful for the takeover of the continent, and fewer men on their side would need to die in battle.

Once Thessian escorted Emilia back to the palace, he stood still and snapped, "Come out, Laurence!"

Laurence's heart nearly jumped out of his chest. He was caught.

Rubbing the back of his neck, Laurence smiled cheerfully as he stepped out of the shadows. "It is a pleasant time for a stroll, wouldn't you agree?"

"Did you hear everything?"

Laurence diverted his eyes off to one side. "I heard enough…"

"You know, eavesdropping on royalty is a crime punishable by death in Hellion."

Laurence laughed nervously. "It is a good thing we are not in the Empire, Your Highness."

Thessian sighed. He drew closer to Laurence and placed his hand on the knight's shoulder. "Do not breathe a word about this."

"If I may be so bold, why not use her power? She could become a greater asset if you were to utilise her ability to the fullest."

"That is not for you to decide." Thessian withdrew his hand and started making his way towards the stables.

"What if someone else figures out her ability and steals her away?"

"Laurence…" The prince's voice had a sharp edge to it.

"You know I am not wrong!"

Thessian turned around. His eyes gleamed with fury. One look at the prince sent a chill down Laurence's back. This was the same face Thessian wore on the battlefield for his enemies. In the fifteen years they had been together, no matter how hard Laurence pushed, His Highness never reacted in such a way.

"She is not an object. Emilia has pledged to help us without the need to forcefully bind her to my side." Thessian relaxed his face, but his hands remained balled at his sides. "You cannot entrap a Seer. Think about it. What is stopping her from giving us false prophecies? I would rather she helped out of her own free will than acted in desperation."

Laurence could not deny the obvious. Mages with the power to *See* were rarer than Dragonite. "Do you think she saw her meeting with you would go smoothly, so that is why she stayed in that tower?"

"We can never know what goes on in the head of someone who can see the future."

"What if she lied? This could be some kind of elaborate ploy to get close to you."

Thessian's face darkened. "Then I will kill her with my own two hands."

Laurence scratched his head. He didn't wish to press the issue any further, because he sensed it could be his head going down the hill along with the prince's boots.

Laurence rode his horse to the Lionhart Guild. He needed answers that night. After tying the horse to the hitching rail next to the guild, he made his way inside. Unlike yesterday, the guild was almost empty. The gamblers were nowhere in sight.

He briefly scanned the large hall for Rime or Jehan. Neither was present. Instead, a woman named Sally operated the reception.

With long strides, he closed the distance between them and leaned his elbow on the oak counter. "Good evening, my lady."

Sally eyed him with suspicion, something he wasn't used to from women. "I remember you, milord. You came here looking for the guild master last night."

He grinned. "Would you be so kind as to arrange a meeting for me?"

Sally did not budge despite his best smile that could charm even the most stubborn of noble women. Instead, she also rested her elbow on the counter and leaned in. He could tell she was using a stool to stand on and match the height of the customers. "He is busy today. Come back another time."

Laurence's smile faded. He straightened up. "Could I meet with someone of similar status?"

"That would be me." Sally mimicked his posture with her small body. "What can I help you with?"

Reluctantly, he pulled out the documents Thessian had given him. "I would like to verify whether this information is correct."

Sally skimmed over the papers and passed them back to him. "They are all legitimate."

"How can you tell?"

"Because these documents were provided by our guild to one of our esteemed customers. We do not provide unverified information as that would destroy our guild's reputation."

Laurence gathered the papers and tucked them into the inner pocket of his cloak. Now that he knew Queen Emilia did not lie to them, his fears came to fruition. Marquess Walden and Prince Thessian's spymaster, who was related to Walden by blood, could not be trusted.

They needed to return to Darkgate as soon as possible.

The problem was that part of Thessian's army was on their way to the Newburn to stabilise the region, the advance of which was loyal and, more importantly, paid by the Marquess. Prince Thessian had not sent any orders to stop them, so their forces should be arriving within the next couple of days via the territories of the lords who supported the coup.

"Would you like a drink before you head out, milord?" Sally asked.

Laurence blinked several times. He had completely forgotten where he was. "There is no need. I should be leaving."

"You should rest," she insisted, pointing to a free table nearby. "You have suddenly turned pale."

"Then, I guess, I will trouble you a while longer." He sat on a solid wood bench as he gathered his thoughts.

In the meantime, Sally brought him a cup of ginger tea and a saucer with honey biscuits. "Here, eat this."

Laurence took a bite. The biscuits weren't half-bad. He reached for his coin purse. "How much do I owe you for the information and the food?"

Sally shook her head. "There is no need for payment. Our

esteemed patron has paid for the information. All I have done is verify it."

"Does your esteemed patron duel the guild master often?"

Sally's brows inched upwards. "You saw that?"

"The commotion caused by such an event was hard to miss."

"That was their first real duel," Sally said with a hint of disappointment. "I wish our guest didn't get hurt."

Laurence sipped his tea. The strong scent of ginger overpowered his sense of smell. "I take it you are aware of her identity and the consequences?"

Sally pressed her lips into a grim line. She inclined her head and walked back to the reception desk.

Once he finished his drink and biscuits, he wiped his mouth as he approached her with an apologetic look on his face. "I did not mean to pry. I am simply surprised by what happened. To be honest, I expected everyone here to be imprisoned for hurting someone of her status. It was foolish of her to get into a duel in the first place."

Sally clicked her tongue and lost any shred of pleasantness as she slapped her hands to her hips. "Lady Em is not a petty person. She is straightforward and honest. Her actions are always well thought out, and she does not discriminate, unlike the other nobles." She pointed to the door. "If your business here is concluded, milord, then please leave."

Laurence sauntered out of the guild.

Sally thought highly of Emilia, enough to defend her.

Maybe the Cursed Princess is not a villain?

He untied his horse and hopped onto the saddle.

Only time will tell.

12
A MESSY SITUATION

THESSIAN

Thessian **stared blankly at the campfire** while he sat on a log. The flames danced to the whims of the breeze that chilled him and his soldiers to the bone. He could not wrap his mind around how difficult life had been for Emilia. She had to hide her powers and was ostracized from birth by her family.

In contrast to her, he had grown up in a loving environment. His parents, although busy with their imperial duties, made time to see their children as often as possible. He had plenty of friends among the knights. Only in recent years had things for him changed. The nobles became cautious around him as if one wrong word to him would make their heads roll. The servants, too, struggled to hide their fear when they saw him with a sword in hand.

Am I that terrifying?

Emilia's warning about Kyros kept nagging at him. They never spent much time together. While Thessian preferred to learn sword fighting with Knight Commander, his younger brother often ventured to the royal library and would not come out until late at night. Only their elder brother, Cain, attempted to form some kind of relationship with them by visiting when he was not attending his classes at the Imperial Academy.

Is Kyros truly my enemy?

One of the messengers approached Thessian. "Your Highness, a message has arrived from the advance forces." He handed Thessian an envelope with a wax seal.

"Thank you." Thessian returned to his tent where he used his dagger to open the letter. He scanned the contents with a sour expression. Marquess Walden was personally tagging along.

Laurence's voice came from outside the tent. "Your Highness, are you asleep?"

Thessian tossed the letter on the table. "No. What is it?"

Laurence peeled back the door. He slipped into the tent and glanced at the discarded letter. "Bad news?"

"Marquess Walden is coming here with the advance forces."

"That is bad news…"

"Why? Did you learn something?"

Laurence returned the documents Emilia had provided. "I visited the local information guild. They told me they were the ones to investigate Walden."

"Do you believe they're trustworthy?" Thessian was beginning to get a headache. He hoped they got it wrong, and Marquess Walden was not in Kyros' pocket.

"They are the only guild around who deals with information. After speaking with a few members, they seem like good people."

Pouring wine into a goblet, Thessian said, "When Walden arrives, we will need to take care of him. Also, hire a new messenger and send them to Darkgate. Have the spymaster and anyone hired by him investigated by Ludwig."

"What about Emilia's problem with the Duke's army?"

"I received word that Duke Malette arrived here with three hundred of his men. They remain stationed outside of the capital for the time being. Send Ronne to watch them. We must know the second they make their move."

Laurence frowned. "Why did the Duke not take his men into the city?"

"It appears, another noble's soldiers were also there on standby, and they came in contact with each other."

"Why would there be so many soldiers waiting beyond Newburn walls, unless they knew about our coup? Could Emilia have arranged for that noble to attack if her negotiations failed?"

Thessian gripped the goblet in his hand. Emilia knew about the invasion but wasn't sure of the outcome. Was the prophecy she saw incomplete? Or had the noble who supported her brought his men in secret? She did mention that her powers were unstable. "Let us deal with Marquess Walden first. Should he suspect we know of his secret dealings with Kyros, he may decide to use his men against us."

"Do you think we can fool him?" Laurence asked as he rested his back against the tent pole. Crossing his arms, he offered, "We could hire some ladies of the night to keep him entertained."

Thessian raised a brow. "Have you become well-acquainted with the local brothels already?"

"Your Highness, I have been slaving away for the past two days, trying to find answers for you, yet you jest in such a terrible way. My feelings are hurt!"

Letting out a chuckle, Thessian said, "Walden won't fall for the petty tricks of a prostitute. He is more interested in lining his pockets with gold. I will deal with him. You will have to help Emilia."

Laurence smirked. "And here I thought you would want to keep that beauty all to yourself."

Thessian looked around the room, spotting his sword resting against a storage chest.

"What are you searching for?" Laurence inquired.

"My sword. I need to cut your tongue out."

Laurence raised his hands and backed out of the tent. "You look tired, Your Highness. I won't bother you any longer."

Taking a seat at the table, Thessian drank his wine and tapped his finger against the hard wood. Ever since Laurence met Emilia, he had not stopped talking about her appearance.

Is Laurence interested in her?

His friend spent many years on the battlefield with Thessian and later helped with the restoration and protection of the Darkgate territory. If Emilia showed signs of liking Laurence back, Thessian may put in a good word for him.

13
DECISIONS DECISIONS

EMILIA

Emilia sat on her bed and blew out a lungful of air. Her shoulders ached as if the weight of the world rested on them. She smacked herself on the forehead and groaned in pain.

How could I lie to him like that?

Ambrose stuck her head around the doorway leading to the bathroom. "Is something bothering you, Your Majesty?"

"I may have told the prince a tiny lie." *Well, it wasn't tiny by any means...*

"Do you believe he will hold it against you if he finds out?"

Emilia's face paled when she recalled how Thessian dealt with betrayal in the novel. "Definitely."

"Should I kill him for you?" Ambrose asked as if she was talking about the monotony of weather and not an assassination of a prince from a powerful nation.

"Don't be ridiculous. You won't be able to get near him."

Ambrose returned to her duties. When she emerged with her sleeves rolled up, she announced, "Your bath is ready. I will assist you out of your garments."

Emilia never did get used to people helping her change. In those moments, she felt like a mannequin instead of a person. Not like she could complain. For the time being, her left shoulder needed a break until her wound healed.

Ambrose skilfully removed Emilia's clothes and helped her get into the bathtub. The bandages had to be removed, which allowed Emilia to take a good look at the damage she sustained.

Ah, this massive burn mark sure is ugly.

Silently, she thanked Sally and Lionhart for their speedy effort to stop the bleeding. Had it not been for them, she would be yet another corpse like in the original story. Though, now that she had changed the main plot's direction, the future would not be the same. It was bound to deviate or become completely different. As long as she could get Thessian on the throne, she would be fine. He would make a good and fair emperor. The support of Hellion's military would grant him a lot of power in the future.

Ambrose gave Emilia's neck a massage that removed the knots she didn't know she had. All stress washed away with the warmth of the lavender-scented water that enveloped her like a cloud of comfort. Her days were only going to get busier. With King Gilebert's funeral being two days away, she could not wait to bury him six feet under. There was also a matter of her giving a speech. She never had given a presentation to more than twenty people in her past life. Soon, she would need to address an entire nation.

Ambrose retracted her hands. "Your Majesty, why did you become tense all of a sudden?"

"I am thinking of useless things again."

After the bath, Ambrose applied the salve gifted by Prince Thessian. Despite slight itching, Emilia could feel the pain lessening and saw the mixture sparkling with magical residue. Why on earth did he give her something that was meant solely for the Hellion royal family? She already felt bad she had deceived him. If they weren't in a novel, she would try to pursue him. Then again, had they met in her world, he would be some rich CEO or son of a president, making it impossible for her to even meet him. Here, she was a person with influence whereas, in her past life, she was a disgraced university student no one cared about.

With Ambrose's help, Emilia climbed under the sheets of her bed.

"I will stay and guard you, Your Majesty."

"I do not believe Duke Malette will attempt another assassination. You should get some sleep, too."

Ambrose knotted her hands in front of her. "It would be unwise to leave you unguarded."

"Don't I have guards outside my room?"

"Aside from Dame Cali Louberte and myself, I would not trust anyone to be able to protect you. Those men may wear the royal guard uniform, but they are working for Count Baudelaire."

"Why have you taken such a liking to the dame?"

"She's foolishly honest and easy to read."

"Why would Prince Thessian assign someone like that to be my guard?" Emilia voiced her inner thoughts.

"Perhaps, he wished to keep you safe."

Emilia dismissed such a possibility. There had to be more to Cali than being overly nice to others. "What did she tell you to make you side with her?"

Ambrose's brows pinched together. "I resonate with her on a certain level. She is of common birth. The local lord wished to take Cali as his wife when she was thirteen, and her parents, who are farmers, did not have the right to refuse. So, she joined the military and became part of Prince Thessian's unit through a rigorous selection process."

"She may, indeed, be foolishly honest or extremely good at lying." From Emilia's experience, it was hard to fool Ambrose. She was a great judge of character and seldom made a mistake. That being said, no one was perfect. No matter how much Emilia wished to believe people at face value, life taught her not to trust anyone. "Have a guild member shadow her in case she drops the act."

"Yes, Your Majesty." Ambrose's fingers toyed with the frills on her apron. "Am I permitted to remain here and guard you?"

Emilia sighed. "Do as you wish."

Ambrose smiled. "Thank you, Your Majesty!"

The next morning, Emilia took her breakfast in her room before heading to her office. She continued to wear black clothes without any accessories. Maintaining the pretence of mourning was hard when she wanted to skip down the long palace halls and throw about confetti. For some reason, the amount of paperwork on her desk was increasing despite the fact she spent most of the previous day working. She groaned when her eyes scanned the big pile next to her.

Was King Gilebert ditching his duties?

She heard her father enjoyed spending his time choosing his next set of jewellery or fine clothes instead of working. No wonder the important paperwork was left to collect dust. The most deplorable act of the king was skipping relief aid to the southern region of Dante.

After a year-long war with the Reyniel Kingdom that led to the farmland becoming useless, the people there were starving to death while the king and his vassals were busy stuffing their hamster cheeks with rare meats and wine. Because of such idiocy, Marquess Rigal turned against the king and sided with Prince Thessian.

She needed to find funds to restore that region and strengthen its military. The kingdom's coffers were almost empty due to the war's end and tribute given to the Reyniel Kingdom. In truth, nothing was stopping Reyniel from attacking again. Since Duke Malette had connections with Reyniel's king, she needed the Duke politically eliminated as soon as possible along with his allies. Then, she could focus on the corruption. If she could shake the fat nobles loose of the money they stole with the help of the king, she could utilise that gold to fill the gap that had formed and help the South.

The guard at the door announced, "Sir Rowell is here to see you, Your Majesty."

"Let him in."

The head butler glided into the room with a tea tray. "I thought Your Majesty would like to take a break from work."

She sighed and sat back in her seat. Ambrose went to the Lionhart Guild, leaving Emilia alone. "Thank you, Sir Rowell."

He set the tray on her desk and prepared the tea in a way that made Emilia stuck for words. His elegant and steady movements were close to a form of art rather than making a simple cup of tea. Such a sight was certainly more interesting than dumping a tea bag in a cup and adding hot water.

He placed the teacup on a saucer in front of her. As he poured the golden liquid into the cup, she could smell chamomile wafting through the air. "I noticed your personal maid was not present and took it upon myself to brew you some tea. This chamomile tea is good for fatigue, Your Majesty."

It seemed the head butler paid close attention to the people around Emilia. Although she was beginning to like him, she had to remain cautious. "It does have a good fragrance."

"I have also brought your new seal and a list of suitable ladies-in-waiting."

Emilia asked him to add two sugars to her tea while she studied the seal in her hand. It was carved out of the elder tree into a shape of a raven. The wood was extremely rare and expensive because it took three hundred years for a single tree to reach maturity. Elder wood had a distinct ebony colour and a natural shine to it. The merchants who wanted to keep the price high had sealed off access to the Elder Forest and burned any trees that grew outside it with the help of the nobles who were in their pocket. "May I ask where you found the materials for this?"

Sir Rowell cleared his throat as he folded his arms behind his back. "I used King Gilebert's old travel chest that was collecting dust in the storage room. I hope I did not overstep my role, Your Majesty."

Emilia put the seal aside and picked up her cup of tea. "Not at all. It is good not to be wasteful." She took a sip and sighed in contentment. "This is a wonderful tea."

"I am pleased you like it." He hesitated for a second before saying, "Would you like any help with choosing your ladies-in-waiting?"

Emilia glanced at the long list of possible candidates. Her knowledge of nobility in Dante extended to the main twenty noble houses and their heads. She paid no attention to the children of those nobles and, therefore, had no idea who would be fitting for the role. "Why do I need to pick them myself? Aren't ladies-in-waiting usually picked through applications rather than my choosing?"

"That used to be the case in the past, Your Majesty. Your great-grandmother, Queen Athela, forcibly made three noble women into her ladies-in-waiting on a whim. To make it possible for his beloved wife, King Gerome passed a law that allows the Queen of Dante to make the decision herself. Once she selects her ladies-in-waiting, invitations will be sent in a form of a royal decree. Those who disobey will be imprisoned for life. The only limits are health and age. The lady-in-waiting cannot be older than fifty or gravely ill."

"Wow, that's..." *Shitty.* "...interesting."

She tapped her finger on the desk as she skimmed the family names, ages, the women's best attributes, skills, social standings, and physical descriptions. She came upon the daughter of Count Baudelaire who was in her late teens. As tempting as it was to get another Baudelaire into the castle, she refrained. The Count probably wouldn't want his only daughter to end up an unwed spinster. Not like Emilia was planning to remain in power for long, but he and the other nobles did not know that. They believed she managed to convince Prince Thessian to spare her life and leave the throne in her capable hands. In the past, Sir Rowell recommended bringing in the daughter of Marchioness Lucienne Durand who was the old king's supporter.

Lifting her gaze from the list, she asked, "How loyal was Marchioness Durand to the king?"

"Her personal goals are unknown to me, Your Majesty. The Marchioness inherited her title with difficulty after her husband died five years ago. During the meetings of the lords, the Marchioness always supported whatever the king wanted. Her family is known to be a part of the royalist faction."

"Would you say she could become my supporter if I take in her youngest daughter?"

"That is this humble servant's guess."

Emilia already had two marquesses from the Southeast on her side, but their military force was nothing compared to Marchioness Durand. Taking a better look at the information, she saw that Lady Christine was fifteen. She had no fiancé and was an average student at the Dante Royal Academy. Her skills were embroidery and drawing. The best class score was for Foreign Literature. Emilia nearly rolled her eyes. Those were great skills for a meek young lady. Maybe, Christine was what Emilia needed.

If the girl was too ambitious, she would act out and become a nuisance. What caught Emilia's eye was a disturbing piece of information in Christine's description. She was raped by her uncle at the age of ten. Lady Christine had no chance at marriage if news of such an event got out.

Emilia felt sick in her stomach and pushed her cup away. "Was that piece of trash ever charged for his crime?"

"Yes, Your Majesty," Sir Rowell replied with a sullen expression. "He was beheaded. The Marchioness took the liberty of doing the deed with her own hands."

"Good!" Her hands shook with anger. "Send Lady Christine Durand an invitation."

Emilia had already extended an invitation to the marchioness for a visit to the palace. Now, she could use Lady Christine as a bargaining chip. Giving Durand's daughter the status of Queen's lady-in-waiting was bound to bring the Durand march to her side.

Emilia smirked. "Anyone else you think would be a good fit for me?"

"Count Alard's eldest daughter is a recent graduate from the Royal Academy. She excels in management."

"Hmm." Count Alard was on her side. He was rather quiet during the honouring ceremony and easy to miss with his plain appearance. He also didn't ask for much. The only thing he wanted was a letter of acceptance from the Royal Academy for his son who failed the entrance exams.

Would he be okay with me stealing his smart daughter?

Emilia read the information about Count Alard's daughter next. She was eighteen, finished her education with honours in Management and Politics, had good fencing skills, and, to Emilia's dismay, had a fiancé. That meant Emilia would be breaking up a possible relationship. "Do you know anything about her engagement?"

"It is a political marriage. Lord Alard could not refuse the offer from Marquess Sole when it came. To avoid marriage, Lady Brianna Alard studied for an extra year at the Royal Academy and is due to marry next month."

"So it's an arranged marriage without love. Perfect. Send her an invitation as well." As an afterthought, she added, "I only want to invite these ladies to work for me. Please inform them that there will be no penalty should they refuse."

"Would you like to consider any other candidates, Your Majesty?"

Her stomach had finally settled enough for her to finish her tea. "Should they decline, I'll select someone else. At the moment, I am more than happy to have my maid and you around. I do not require additional help."

"Thank you for your praise, Your Majesty." He bowed. "I will make arrangements for the invitations to be delivered swiftly."

"How are the funeral arrangements coming along?"

"There is an issue of the number of soldiers who can guard Your Majesty. As most of the guards would need to be stationed around the city and the palace, there may be gaps in your protection."

Emilia didn't want to reveal to others that she could fight. The lords underestimating her abilities was a trump card she wanted to keep for as long as possible. She was also injured.

Although Thessian's and the royal physician's treatments were keeping the pain at a manageable level, she wouldn't be able to use her arm for another two months. In hindsight, she was regretting her recklessness.

"Should I summon Dame Cali Louberte for you to discuss tomorrow's security?" he asked.

"Yes, that would be good."

The guard at the door knocked. "Sir Laurence is here to see you, Your Majesty."

"Let him in." She turned to Sir Rowell. "Could you bring some tea and refreshments for my guest and send a summons to Count Baudelaire? He should be staying in his manor in the city."

Sir Rowell inclined his head. "Yes, Your Majesty."

He backed out of the room as Sir Laurence waltzed in, dressed in a nobleman's attire. That look suited him more than the mercenary disguise.

After bowing in greeting, Sir Laurence beamed at her with a smile that could make the heart of a virgin maiden explode. Luckily, his charms were wasted on her. She knew how dangerous he was behind that playful mask. He was the second-best swordsman in the Hellion Empire, after Prince Thessian.

"Greetings, Your Majesty. I was sent by His Highness." He placed his hand over his chest. "Please use my body as you wish."

Emilia highly doubted Thessian sent Laurence as a plaything for the queen. Such suggestive talk was a test. Rising from her chair, she made her way around her desk and stopped a short distance away from him.

Lifting her head to meet his dark gaze, she asked, "Are you saying, Sir Laurence, I can do anything I want with you?"

He smirked. "Of course, Your Majesty."

She smiled back at him. "That is wonderful news! I was short on security for tomorrow's funeral. You have come at the perfect time. Your body will, indeed, be of good use."

His smile withered. "I am merely above average with the sword. Surely, others are more suited to escort you."

"Nonsense," she countered, "I have heard plenty of tales about Prince Thessian's heroism on the battlefield. His second-in-command must be just as good."

Sir Laurence raised a brow. "What kind of tales did you hear?"

"I heard he defeated one hundred soldiers all by himself."

"You were misinformed, Your Majesty."

"Oh?"

He grinned. "It was the two of us, and two hundred."

Emilia couldn't restrain her chuckle. According to the original story, Thessian and Sir Laurence got separated from the main forces and were attacked by twenty bandits. The story got embellished and exaggerated by Sir Laurence when he attended the balls thereafter. Not like she could tell him she knew the truth.

He eyed her with interest. "What is so funny? Do you know I am lying because you *saw* the fight?"

She stepped back and narrowed her eyes. *Did Thessian tell him about my ability? No. He wouldn't have. He swore an oath on his name, and Thessian always keeps his word.* The only other conclusion was obvious. "Eavesdropping on royalty is a terrible offence, Sir Laurence."

"That is exactly what my master told me."

"I see that he did not discipline you, either."

Laurence rubbed the back of his neck awkwardly. "I will keep it a secret. There is no need to worry."

"I know you will." Emilia motioned to the two cushy baby-blue sofas in her office that were made by the finest craftsmen in the kingdom. "Please, take a seat. My butler will arrive with tea shortly." She sat down, doing her best not to show any discomfort from her shoulder.

He complied and lowered his body onto the plush seat across from her. Resting his hands on his knees, he said, "I must admit, I cannot fathom your goal. Why are you helping the prince?"

"I think he is a good man."

"That's all?"

"Do I need another reason?"

He thought about it for a second and laughed. "I guess not."

Emilia neatly folded her hands in her lap. "Will you join my security detail tomorrow?"

"It would be my honour." He gave her a cheeky smile.

"You will need to disguise yourself as one of the royal guards. Dame Cali will provide you with the uniform."

"I heard you assigned her to a new post." Sir Laurence seemed unhappy with her decision. "Prince Thessian wanted Cali to be your guard."

"She will return to her original duty once the palace guards have been organised, and I find someone more suitable for the job. After the coup, as you well know, there has been a shortage of guards because they have all been killed. Not that I blame His Highness, of course."

"We have provided forty men to protect the palace in the meantime. Shouldn't that be enough?"

"You are forgetting the knights that were brought in by my vassal, Count Baudelaire. They see your men as mercenaries who should not be anywhere near the palace. That is why I need someone like Dame Cali to mediate between the two factions."

Sir Rowell brought more tea along with refreshments. He arranged the food on the tea table and handed a cup on a saucer to Emilia. Then, he proceeded to make one for Sir Laurence who was busy munching on the biscuits.

Once Cali arrived, the conversation shifted to the guard stationing during the funeral parade and the slight increase in crime as the city guards' numbers had dwindled.

Emilia lost interest after a while and stared out of the window of her office, spotting a grey owl sitting on a tree branch. In her past life, Eastern Europeans and Native Americans considered owls as bad omens or associated them with death. She made a mental note to carry a dagger with her tomorrow, just in case.

14
MARQUESS' ARRIVAL

THESSIAN

Thessian did not get any sleep that night. The moment the sun peeked over the horizon; he left his tent to train. Stress was a beast he fought daily.

His sword instructor used to say, 'When the body works, the mind rests.'

After years of swinging the sword and improving his physique, Thessian wholeheartedly agreed. The matter of Marquess Walden had to be handled with utmost care.

Sweat ran down his back and chest. Despite the cold weather, his body burned like a roaring fire. He wiped the sweat off his brow when he sensed the presence of another. Turning around, he noticed Renne standing under a tree with her hands at her sides and her hood covering her head. Renne was Ronne's twin sister, and it was sometimes hard to tell them apart, especially when they wore the same hairstyle and clothes. Thessian came upon them as children during the war. To that day, he believed he made the right decision to keep them by his side. Their hard work and efficiency in gathering and delivering information helped him out countless times.

Now, as a spirited fifteen-year-old, Renne saluted him. "Your Highness, Marquess Walden will arrive within the hour. He is bringing his guards with him."

"How many?"

"I counted twelve in total."

Not many. Thessian's camp had enough men to take care of them if a fight broke out. "Has the rest of our unit been alerted to the plan?"

"Yes, Your Highness."

Thessian lifted his tired eyes to the cloudless sky. He hoped the gods were on his side and would spare him too many losses. "I will wash up and get changed. When Marquess Walden arrives, bring him to my tent."

She placed her hand over her heart and bowed. Without another sound, Renne was gone like a mirage.

Thessian ran his hand over his face. Ludwig taught those children too well. Over the past year, he had received dozens of complaints from his knights that the twins startled them by popping out of nowhere. He may need to ask them to make some noise while they're at the camp for the benefit of his soldiers' hearts.

After a quick wash in the stream nearby, he returned to his tent. He had not worn Hellion colours ever since they had set out for Dante. Being dressed in white and red again made him miss his home. He glanced around, making sure everything had been prepared perfectly. Now, he needed to keep the Marquess occupied.

From the other side of the tent door, Renne announced, "Your Highness, Marquess Walden has arrived and wishes to speak with you."

"Escort him inside."

Renne peeled back the door, and Marquess Walden marched in

as if he owned the place with his trusted knight at his side. Dressed in a grey fur coat and with his salt and pepper hair, Walden reminded Thessian of a raccoon. The prince inwardly wondered how he had missed Walden's self-important attitude before. Was he blinded by the fact his father trusted this marquess? He would not make the same mistake again thanks to Emilia.

"Marquess Walden, it has been a while." Thessian kept his tone neutral yet pleasant as he sat down at the table full of food and drink. He motioned to the seat opposite him. "Come and join me for breakfast."

The Marquess huffed a greeting as he bowed and assumed his seat. "I came here—"

Thessian narrowed his eyes. "We can discuss business after the meal. Or are you in such a hurry that I must be deprived of my breakfast after my morning training session?"

The Marquess frantically waved his hands in front of his face. "I would not dare, Your Highness!"

"Renne, pour our guest some ale and set the table for him. He must be parched after such a rushed journey here."

Renne picked up a ceramic jug and poured Marquess Walden a drink. In a fashion befitting of a palace maid, she arranged the cutlery and a plate in front of the Marquess. She then stepped to one side and folded her hands behind her back, keeping her eyes trained on the floor.

Thessian raised his goblet. "I hope you will like this ale. Sir Laurence could not stop singing its praises, so we had to purchase a barrel."

"Yes, I am sure it tastes wonderful," Walden mumbled and swallowed a mouthful.

"How was your journey here?" Thessian calmly ate his food, occasionally pausing to drink his ale. "I did not expect you to come here personally with the advance forces."

"I was merely concerned for Your Highness' safety. Because I heard no news about how the coup went, I rushed out here to make sure you were unscathed."

It had barely been a few days since the king's death. Usually, it took two weeks to march to Newburn from Darkgate. *How did Walden make it in such a short time? Surely, he left shortly after me and was waiting nearby.* "As you can see, I am in perfect health."

"It would appear so."

Is that disappointment in this weasel's tone? Thessian smirked. "I am pleased to have such a caring ally on my side."

"Of course. My loyalty lies only with you, my prince."

Thessian itched to use his sword on the Marquess' neck. Walden was acting as if he wasn't serving two masters at the same time while reaping all the benefits.

As hard as it was to maintain his composure, Thessian managed it and kept eating for as long as possible. Before the meal, Renne mixed in some sleeping powder with the ale. Thessian had taken the antidote, but he could faintly feel its effect.

When he noticed Marquess Walden was getting slower at his flattery, Thessian said, "I believe it is time to discuss business." He glanced at Walden's knight. "In private."

Walden rubbed his hands together. "Yes, of course. Sir Hainz, wait outside."

The knight bowed his head and stepped out, followed by Renne who didn't need a command from Thessian.

"Now that we are alone," Thessian began as he wiped his mouth with a napkin. "Would you care to tell me why you are receiving bribes from my brother?"

The Marquess blanched. "Wha-what nonsense are you saying?"

Thessian moved at once, pressing the edge of his dagger to Walden's throat. His eyes blazed with pent-up fury. "You foul man. Do you dare deny your deeds?"

"I-I would neve—"

Pressing the blade harder against Walden's skin, Thessian drew blood.

Walden must have realised the prince was serious because he swallowed nervously. "I-I have committed a grave sin, Your Highness."

"So, you finally remembered how much I hate liars?"

"Your Highness, please remove the blade, and I will explain

everything."

Thessian sat on the edge of the table and planted his boot between Walden's legs. He leant in while keeping the dagger in place. "You dare to order me around?"

"No! No, I merely—"

"What were you planning once you became regent?"

Walden glared at the prince. His mask finally slipped. "Prince Kyros was right. You are unworthy of the throne. You behave like a savage beast that's let loose from its cage."

"Oh? Is that how my dear brother sees me? A mindless beast?" Thessian let out a bitter laugh.

For how many years had he believed there was no animosity between him and his brothers? They were given equal opportunities by their father and excelled in different things. Yet, to be called a *beast*? He had never once done anything to offend Kyros.

So why?

Did Kyros' desire for the throne make him forget about his family ties? "Speak! What was your plan?"

"As if I would tell you..." Walden's eyes began to lose their focus. Thessian was running out of time. The mandragora root was taking effect. "You are nothing but a brainless brute with no future!" With that, the Marquess landed face-first into his half-eaten fish fillet.

Thessian had withdrawn his leg and dagger, preventing further injury to the marquess as he fell. He could not kill Walden outright. His father would need justification for such an act. Even physical torture was off the table to get the answers out of him. For the time being, all he could do was bide his time while keeping Marquess Walden under his watchful eye.

Thessian checked Walden's pulse, making sure he was out cold, and left the tent. Outside, the knights who had escorted the Marquess were knocked out and tied up.

Thessian's men all stood to attention on his arrival.

Renne rushed over and placed her hand over her chest. "Your Highness, Marquess Walden's soldiers have been subdued. What would you have me do next?"

"Secure the Marquess and keep an eye on him. You have permission to use anything you want to extract information out of him as long as he remains physically intact."

Her lips spread into a gleeful smile that unsettled even Thessian when it appeared. "Could I test my new concoction on him?"

"Be my guest."

***

The entire afternoon, Thessian was busy planning his next move. To eliminate Walden's men from the advance force, he had to act fast. He ordered his knights to purchase a large amount of ale from Newburn's taverns and had them add the sleeping drug to each barrel.

As he headed for his tent, Renne came out and ran over to him. "Your Highness, I have his confession."

"What did he say?"

She looked around. "Would you prefer to hear this in private?"

Thessian led the way to a small clearing where he often trained. He faced her and crossed his arms over his chest. "Speak."

"Marquess Walden was colluding with Prince Kyros to take over the Dante Kingdom. Over time, they were planning on building an uprising which you would be forced to deal with personally."

He tilted his head to one side in confusion. "How would they do that?"

"It is your territory, Your Highness. The Marquess was going to feign an illness and see to it that you were the one to quell the rebellion."

Rubbing his chin in thought, he asked, "Anything else?"

"He was surprised to hear about the princess' survival. I do not believe she is involved in their plan."

"Yes. She has warned me multiple times to be wary of my

brother. I should return her kindness." He never wanted things to escalate to the point of bloodshed, but if that was what Kyros wanted, Thessian had no choice.

The tilt of Renne's head made her shoulder-length, chestnut-coloured hair shine in the sunlight. "What would you have me do with the Marquess?"

"Arrange for an escort and bring him to the Dark Tower, discreetly. We can later claim he died in battle. When you arrive in Darkgate, trust only Ludwig and do not use old messengers."

"I understand, Your Highness."

"Before you leave, get rid of Walden's guards. We have no use for them."

Renne bowed. "I will inform Your Highness when we cross the northern border." With a serious look unfit for a child her age, she sped off to assume her duties.

Thessian ran his hand over his face. Once more, he hesitated to start a real fight for the throne with Kyros. Was there a misunderstanding between them he needed to clear up? Deep down, he knew Kyros had distanced himself from Thessian and Cain since they were children. While Cain was away at the Imperial Academy, Thessian kept up with his sword training and sparred with the knights. Kyros ignored any attempts his brothers made to spend time together. Instead, he hid in the Imperial Library from dusk till dawn as if searching for something.

What exactly was Kyros up to back then? More importantly, why is that bothering me now?

15
UNDERTONES

EMILIA

Emilia's head hurt from the amount of paperwork she had to read during the day. She took a break by lying on top of the sofa in her office and staring at the sculpted ceiling. Whoever designed it had to be a fan of naked women in goddess-like poses.

Oh well. Not like she could complain that she wished the sculptures were half-naked men with endless rows of abdominal muscles. The servants would think she lost her mind to depravity. Though, secretly, the maids were probably imagining the same things. She had, more than on one occasion, overheard them discussing the knights who trained without their shirts on. In the future, she may need to attend the training. To supervise the men, of course.

"What an unladylike way of resting, Your Majesty," Sir Laurence commented from his post by the door. He had settled in her office as her guard and even found the time to change into the royal guard's uniform. Oddly enough, the silver and blue colours suited his regal face.

"I am a perfect lady when I need to be." Emilia contemplated what he would look like wearing the Empire's formal uniform. She heard their buckles were made of pure gold and their ceremonial swords were more expensive than a house.

"You certainly have my master fooled."

"I highly doubt anyone can fool His Highness."

The now-familiar knock came from the door, and Sir Rowell entered the room. He did not show any reaction when he saw her sprawled out on the sofa like a log. Over the years, as the head butler, he must have seen quite a lot of strange things. "Your Majesty, Count Baudelaire wishes to have an audience with you."

She forced her body into a sitting position with a groan. Once the ache in her shoulder subsided, she said, "Let him in and bring some refreshments."

"Yes, Your Majesty." Sir Rowell guided the Count inside.

Emilia smiled pleasantly. "Count Baudelaire, thank you for coming to see me."

The Count bowed in greeting and returned her smile. "I am pleased to be of assistance, Your Majesty."

"Do take a seat." She motioned to the seats across from her.

Baudelaire accepted her invitation and sat down. He neatly folded his hands in his lap. "I heard you were attacked by an assassin."

"Yes. Duke Malette is eager to be rid of me." She gauged his reaction which seemed to reflect sympathy and a hint of pity. In his eyes, she must have looked like a helpless young girl with the weight of a kingdom on her shoulders. "No need to worry, Lord Baudelaire. The physician said I will make a full recovery in two months."

"That is good to hear."

"I called you here to ask for your help once more." Emilia knotted her hands in her lap and met his steady gaze. "I wish to ask for your assistance during the funeral procession. As you may have guessed, the castle is currently understaffed in terms of security. Although you have graciously provided me with forty of your guards, along with the ones I have, they may not be enough to cover the palace and the route to the temple."

"I see what you mean... I have three hundred men stationed outside the city walls. If you grant your permission, I will have them enter and guard you during the parade."

"Three hundred is too grand a number for me."

The trip from the palace to the temple was a mere five kilometres. She didn't want to make it seem like the Count was pulling the strings behind her reign. If possible, she wanted to rely as little as possible on the large noble houses that could easily topple her while she and the palace were in a vulnerable state.

Once the year's taxes from the nobles came in, and Duke Malette was dealt with, she was going to ask Dame Cali to begin the recruitment process for the palace guards and Emilia's personal knights. Remaining at the mercy of the nobles was foolish.

"Are you hesitating because you do not trust me, Your Majesty?" The Count's straightforward question was a rarity in a world where everyone layered their sentences with pointless pleasantries and hidden jabs.

Emilia managed to keep her expression neutral. "Besides Duke Malette, I am the only remaining member of the royal bloodline. You must understand why I am being cautious."

He chuckled. "I understand your worry about placing your trust in a single noble house but—" He got up and went down on one knee in front of her. After lowering his head, he added, "I, Count Edmund Augustine Baudelaire, and the Baudelaire House give our allegiance to the rightful heir and Queen of Dante." He raised his head enough for her to see the sincerity in his grey eyes that were framed by deep wrinkles. "All I ask is that you become a just ruler the people of Dante deserve."

Emilia felt her cheeks reddening. That was the first time someone had pledged unwavering loyalty in such a formal way. "Please rise, Lord Baudelaire. You must be uncomfortable."

He let out a hearty laugh as he sluggishly climbed to his full height. "These old bones may be creaky, but I can still bend the knee when it is required. And, please, feel free to call me Edmund, Your Majesty."

"I did not expect you to do that."

"I did not plan to at first," he admitted, returning to his seat. "But there is something about you that gives this old man hope that smiles will one day return to the faces of this nation."

She placed her hand over her heart. "I swear, I will do everything in my power to fulfil your wish, with your guidance, of course."

"You give me too much credit. I have a feeling you already have a lot of things planned for Dante."

She couldn't hide her smile. "Many things will need to be changed. Because of that, I fear many nobles will push back against my decisions."

"House Baudelaire will become your shield, Your Majesty. I have spent a lifetime making my fortune. I may as well invest it now."

Sir Rowell arrived with the tea and carrot cake.

The rest of the conversation between Emilia and the Count became more light-hearted as they discussed the current trends among the nobility and their newfound interest in luxury goods imported from the Hellion Empire.

In the end, she got up from her seat. "It was a pleasure to have you here, Edmund. I hope you will coordinate with the Guard Captain regarding tomorrow's event. You also have my permission to let one hundred of your men into the city."

"Thank you, Your Majesty."

Once the Count was out of her office, Emilia glanced over her shoulder at Sir Laurence who seemed to be deep in thought.

She smirked. "See? I can be ladylike when needed."

His seriousness melted away in a split second. "I doubt that old man would have lowered himself like that if he knew you were Hellion's chess piece."

Emilia held in her retort by tightening her jaw. He wasn't wrong. She chose the hard path. She wanted to keep Prince Kyros from becoming emperor. "I truly hope your disease gets cured one day."

"What disease?"

"Only the greatest of scholars will know. Now, please leave me alone. I wish to work in peace."

He huffed, "I will be outside."

When the sun set and the fires were lit in the fireplaces throughout the palace, Emilia yawned and rubbed her stinging eyes. She had greatly underestimated the amount of work that needed to be done. She was beginning to think King Gilebert never visited his office in the first place. He had abandoned many useful projects and even sold logging rights of the Southern Forest to Reyniel's king without negotiating with Marquess Rigal first. She wanted to bang her head against her desk. Maybe that would make things seem more like a dream.

"This is an admin's nightmare," she said as she looked out of her office window.

The creepy owl was gone, and the sky was completely black, matching the colour of her dress. She was beginning to grow tired of the dresses. As someone from the Modern Age, she wanted to wear some baggy jeans and a comfy sweater while she caught up on her favourite TV shows. TV was not something available to her. The Dante Kingdom was so far behind on technology that she was amazed they had running water in the palace. Even that, they learned from the Hellion Empire that had been engulfing the continent, one kingdom at a time. She missed hot showers as well. Not having to wait for a bath to be ready would save time in her schedule for other things.

Someone cleared their throat. "Your Majesty?"

She turned around, finding Sir Rowell and Ambrose waiting. "I didn't hear you two come in."

"We called multiple times," Sir Rowell commented. "May I ask, how is your speech for tomorrow coming along?"

Speech?

Emilia had completely forgotten to write one. "Can I not just weep into a handkerchief and pretend to be heartbroken?"

Ambrose hid her snickering behind a light cough.

Sir Rowell gave Emilia a stern look. "Your Majesty will be addressing the noble houses in attendance. You must prepare a suitable speech to make them acknowledge you as the true successor of the crown."

"You are right, Sir Rowell. I must put forward my best acting." Emilia returned to her desk. "Ambrose, could you give me a massage? My shoulders are stiff from sitting all day."

The maid moved behind Emilia and gently placed her hands on the Queen's shoulders. With fingers crafted by God himself, or so Emilia thought every time Ambrose laid her hands on Emilia's body, the pleasant experience she needed began. Ambrose even avoided the wound as best she could.

"I will return in an hour," Sir Rowell informed with a bow. "Should you need any help with the speech, I will be available all night, Your Majesty."

Emilia almost moaned when Ambrose hit the right spot. "Great."

When he shuffled out, Emilia lifted her head and peeked at Ambrose. "Do you think he is becoming bold?"

"The head butler?"

"Yes. He is even scolding me now."

"Should I kill him?"

Emilia laughed. "That won't be necessary." She picked up a fountain pen and selected a blank sheet of parchment. "How did it go at the guild?"

Ambrose lowered her voice so only Emilia could hear her. "Lionhart will plant eyes next to the Duke and his men who have remained in the city, as per your request. He will notify you should an escape attempt take place during the funeral."

"Did he say when he will assume his role as my spymaster?"

"He mentioned it will happen sometime after the funeral. He

also said that until then, the Lionhart Guild is at your disposal."

Emilia stretched out her neck, allowing Ambrose's hands better access to her tired muscles. "At least, he is not packing up to run away. I half-expected him to ignore me."

"Lionhart's honour is important to him, Your Majesty."

"Alright. I best get started on my tear-jerking speech. You can rest in the meantime."

Ambrose stepped away from Emilia. "I will remain by your side until you need me."

Emilia pointed to the sofa. "Take a break, Ambrose. You have been running around all day. You need to rest as well."

"But you—"

"No buts. Rest!"

"I understand." Ambrose stiffly plopped onto the sofa. She must have been exhausted, because she fell asleep sitting upright after five minutes of doing nothing.

16
TRUE MOTIVES

LAURENCE

Laurence escorted Emilia to her bedchambers after she finished work for the day. Although she was a regent serving Prince Thessian, she seemed to be fulfilling her duty diligently.

He couldn't wrap his head around her intentions. *Why would she go so far for a kingdom that gave her nothing?*

Laurence scanned the long, empty hallway. The Queen had no other guards all day long.

Why?

If he was in her position, he would have assigned at least a dozen to watch his back. The only reason to limit the number of people around her was out of lack of trust. He nodded to himself as if he finally glimpsed a piece of her true motives.

Yes. That has to be it.

Giving the hallway one more look, he left his post to find Cali.

She had completely forgotten her mission, and he needed to remind her that her master had not changed.

It didn't take long to find his subordinate. Cali was in the armoury, taking stock of the weapons. Laurence rested his shoulder against the door frame and cleared his throat.

Cali turned her head. Upon seeing him there, her expression brightened. "Captain! What can I do for you?"

"Oh, you still remember who your superiors are?"

She frowned. "I do not understand."

He pushed away from the frame and strode over to her. "What is your mission, Dame Calithea Louberte?"

In the blink of an eye, she stood to attention. "To protect Queen Emilia and keep an eye on the people she meets."

"And what are you doing?"

Cali lowered her head in shame. "I am acting as a temporary Guard Captain, Commander."

"Remember who you serve, Cali. Another mistake, and you will be kicked out of the elite unit."

"What would you have me do?"

He patted her on the shoulder. "Maintain your current position. I'll guard the Queen. When I return to Prince Thessian's side, you will resume your post as her guard."

"Understood."

Laurence was ready to dismiss her but paused. "Do I look sick to you?"

Her eyes widened with worry as she scanned every inch of him. "No, sir."

"Hmm." Could he truly be sick, like Emilia said? He could run for ten miles without stopping for a break and keep up with his daily training.

Unless... Is it not a visible disease? Did Emilia See me on my deathbed?

Laurence shuddered. Maybe he needed to start thinking about marriage and offspring as his father had mentioned in his last letter.

"Do you feel unwell?" Cali asked.

"No. Do not worry about it. Return to your duties."

With her shoulders slumping, Cali reluctantly resumed counting the swords.

Laurence had to remind himself that dating within the unit would be problematic. It was obvious that Cali liked him, but he had to keep a professional distance between them. Though, not like he could return her affection. She was like a younger sister to him who needed guidance. Romance was not on the table.

17
LIVES OF THE FALLEN

THESSIAN

One could see the fires of the camp set up by the advance forces from miles away. Followed by his men, Thessian rode his horse. Their tension was palpable. It was not long before they were banding together with Marquess Walden. Today, they stood on opposing sides.

The cold air whipped by, making his cape flutter behind him. He suppressed a shiver as the frosty air bit into his face and hands.

One of the commanding officers of the advance force promptly arrived to greet him. "Your Highness, we did not expect you to come by so late."

Thessian motioned to the waggon full of barrels of ale. "Then all this would go to waste."

The commanding officer's eyes bulged. "You are too kind, Your Highness!"

"Think nothing of it and help bring the drink to our exhausted men."

With a quick bow, the commanding officer sped off.

The spirits of the camp lifted rapidly at the sight of alcohol. Cheers and excited hoots from soldiers echoed into the night as they sang merry songs around the campfires with pitchers of ale ready to be emptied.

Thessian pretended to drink with them. He could not let Walden's men suspect something was amiss.

One of Walden's loyal commanders came up to Thessian. "Your Highness, where did the Marquess go?"

"He went on ahead to the castle," Thessian replied.

"Does that mean the initial stage of the coup was a success?"

"Yes."

The man blew out a sigh of relief. "That is wonderful news. Marquess Walden was looking forward to taking charge."

I bet he was. "Tomorrow, we will march on the capital. Go and enjoy yourself with your men."

"Yes, of course, Your Highness."

An hour crept by slower than ever. Thessian was beginning to wonder if his men added enough of the sleeping drug to the alcohol as the merriment was showing hardly any signs of slowing. Then, as if a candle was extinguished, the soldiers began to doze off one by one. Some toppled over others and fell face-first onto the hardened dirt.

"What's happening?" someone shouted.

"Are we under attack?" another yelled.

Thessian nodded to his men to spread out and cull those who did not succumb to the effects of the drug. His soldiers from the advance force also did their part by tying up the unconscious soldiers.

Walking through the mess of sleeping bodies, the prince wondered how many of these men were truly loyal to Walden and how many were there to earn a living for their families. But no good general let the enemy live and not regretted it later.

A scent of blood mixed with smoke filled the air. That familiar stench reminded him of his years on the battlefield where lives were worth as much as a grain of sand in a desert.

Thessian's subordinate arrived at his side. "Your Highness, we have completed the sweep of the camp and secured the Marquess' men. We are checking the surrounding area for anyone who may have been misplaced. What would you have us do?"

"Kill them quickly. That is the only mercy I can grant them."

"I will pass on your order." The knight scurried off.

Sounds of swords slashing at the bodies replaced those of short-lived happiness. Thessian briefly closed his eyes and silently said a prayer for the deceased. As he was on the last verse, he heard a twig snapping in the nearby treeline. His head turned in the direction of the sound.

Someone managed to escape.

There was no time to get his men to search the small forest. So, he broke into a sprint, heading towards the noise. His eyes could faintly make out a hooded figure who was scrambling away from him through the dark, uneven terrain.

Thessian pressed on, feeling the cold air stabbing at his lungs like needles.

The person of small build tripped over an exposed tree root and fell with a high-pitched cry.

Pulling out his sword, Thessian advanced on the enemy. He pointed the blade to where the person's throat would be. It was hard to tell a man from a woman in the dark. The sole light that reached that far into the forest was from the now-distant campfires.

"Remove your hood!" Thessian ordered.

With shaky, pale hands, the person complied. Their wrists appeared to be thin and delicate.

Once the face was exposed, Thessian grabbed them by the arm and dragged them out of the forest and closer to the camp, where he could make out the face better.

His eyes widened in recognition. "Lady Diane Walden, what are you doing here?"

Through rivers of tears streaming down her pale cheeks, she glowered at him. As the youngest daughter of Marquess Walden, she must have pestered her father to let her come along in a bid to win Thessian's heart. "Why are you doing this, Your Highness? Where is my father? Did...did you kill him?"

Thessian hated dealing with noble women the most. Where was Laurence when he needed him? Killing the soldiers was one thing, but killing a woman of nobility would cause him a headache later. He cursed under his breath. "He is alive and well."

"How can I believe you after what I saw here?" She tried to shake his iron grip on her wrist. Using her dainty foot, she stomped on his boot multiple times and even bit his hand.

He narrowed his eyes on her, and she shrunk away. Fear was an expression he had grown used to. The lady was like a caged animal with no survival instincts of her own.

"Your Highness?" Sir Ian, one of Thessian's best archers, ran over to them. "Oh..."

Thessian threw the girl into the knight's arms. "Restrain Lady Diane and keep her quiet until I figure out what to do with her."

The headache Thessian wanted to avoid by getting rid of anything related to the Marquess was going to be impossible now that Lady Diane was involved. Thessian looked in the direction of Emilia's castle. He could ride there with the girl and arrive by dawn.

Emilia may have had a vision of Diane's fate or...

He stopped his train of thought. Using Emilia's powers for something so insignificant could strain their future working relationship. Since Emilia did not warn him about Diane coming with Walden meant the young lady was no threat to them.

Torn over his decision, he opted to take Diane with him to the castle anyway. If not Emilia, surely Laurence would be able to control a single noble lady.

18
WIGGLING BAGGAGE

EMILIA

At four in the morning, Emilia's much-needed sleep was disturbed. She yawned as she sat up in her bed with Ambrose's help and looked at a dishevelled Prince Thessian who stood in the doorway of her bedchambers with a tied-up, flailing woman thrown over his shoulder.

"We should stop meeting in my room in the middle of the night, Your Highness," Emilia grumbled. "Unless you plan to take responsibility for me."

He grimaced as if he had just realised what he had done. "I was in a hurry…"

Emilia's attention did not leave the present he brought. "What is with the luggage? Is it a new maid?"

He lowered the girl who couldn't be older than Emilia onto the floor. The noble lady's expensive bespoke navy-blue dress and sapphire jewellery were hard to miss. "This is Lady Diane Walden, daughter of Marquess Walden."

Diane was ignored by Thessian in the original story, so she only appeared once or twice alongside her father. Now that Emilia's sleepiness had been replaced with complete awareness of the situation, she realised she had made a huge blunder by forgetting an insignificant character. "And what would you have me do with Lady Diane at this hour?"

He crossed his arms. "I would like for you to keep an eye on her."

Emilia covered her eyes with her hand. Was he asking her to babysit a noble's daughter on the day of her family's funeral?

Ambrose bent down and whispered in Emilia's ear, "Should I throw her in the dungeon?"

That wasn't a bad idea, but Emilia doubted the prince wanted a noble of the Empire to be mistreated. Otherwise, he wouldn't come to Emilia's bedroom in such a fashion and present Lady Diane like some wild boar he had caught on a hunt.

"Ambrose, take the lady to a guest room and make sure she stays there, then inform Sir Rowell to attend to her personally. Tell him to be discreet."

"Yes, Your Majesty." Ambrose strode over to Lady Diane.

Without standing on ceremony, Ambrose gripped the girl around the back of her neck and whispered something in Diane's ear that had the young woman stiffen.

Lady Diane left the room without putting up a fight.

Thessian watched the whole situation in amazement. "What did your maid tell her?"

"I think the more pressing issue here is Your Highness waltzing into my room unannounced every night."

He raised his hands in defence. "I thought you would be expecting us."

She rolled her eyes. "I told you my ability is not stable. I cannot see the future whenever I feel like it."

"Yes, I recall."

She raised her chin in defiance. "I expect an apology."

"I am sorry."

"At least you can admit when you're wrong." She climbed out of bed with much effort and pointed at her cape. "Could you help me put it on?"

Thessian raised his brows when he saw her standing in a thin nightgown. It took him several seconds to move and follow her instructions. As he draped the cape around her small body, she looked at his handsome face.

Every one of his fans is probably super jealous right now. Why did the author have to kill him off when he is so good-looking? I'm not drooling, am I? Emilia stealthily checked the corners of her mouth.

"I truly am sorry for rousing you at this hour." He told her while focusing his attention on securing the cape with a pin.

Once she hid her state of undress, she touched one of his callused hands before he had the chance to retract it. "If you are that apologetic, could you do me a favour?"

"What would that be?"

She inched closer and lowered her voice in case someone was listening. "I want you to share your secret stash with me."

As if struck by lightning, he jerked away from her. "How did you know about that?"

She pointed to her temple, implying she saw it in a vision. Though, the truth was that she had always wanted to try the homemade alcohol the prince brewed in his spare time. Not even Laurence had the opportunity to taste it. If true to the story, it tasted like liquid bliss with sweet undertones. The author even compared it to ambrosia made by the gods.

"This is rather embarrassing…"

She smirked. "Will you do me this favour?"

"Only if you promise to take this secret to your grave."

"I would never dare say it out loud, especially not to Sir Laurence." She crossed her heart. "You have my word."

Thessian smiled for the first time since his arrival in her room that night. "I never expected us to share our most intimate secrets when we made that deal in your tower."

Emilia returned his smile with one of her own. "Indeed." She peered past him. "What happened to Sir Laurence?"

"I sent him on an errand."

"What kind of errand?"

"He went to the city to pick out some clothes suitable for Lady Diane during her stay here."

Emilia let out a laugh at the image of Laurence shopping for women's clothes. Many noble women would have their hearts broken if they saw such a sight. "Did you tell him the stores may not be open due to the funeral parade?"

"...I may have forgotten about that."

Emilia was beginning to like Prince Thessian more and more.

19
HAND-ME-DOWNS

LAURENCE

The clock tower's chimes rang throughout the streets of Newburn, informing Laurence that morning had arrived. The simple decorations for the funeral procession, with Dante's national colours and emblem, had been scattered along Main Street, which Queen Emilia would travel on in a couple of hours. Even now, the streets were slowly coming alive with people arriving for the event and stalls opening, brimming with goods to be sold.

The final destination for the procession was the Temple of Holy Light on a hill outside of Newburn. Laurence wondered how the priests were going to react to Emilia showing up on their doorstep.

On the other hand, Prince Thessian must have lost his mind, sending Laurence in the middle of the night in search of dresses for Walden's daughter.

What is that spoiled brat doing here in the first place?

Marquess Walden was too soft on his daughter, which brought about her current unfortunate circumstances. Laurence disliked Lady Diane for many reasons. She was a lady in name only and a vicious viper underneath her mask. When she thought Prince Thessian wasn't looking, she often struck her servants and made them do unreasonable things such as using them as footstools. Just thinking about putting up with that witch made Laurence's insides churn.

He banged on the door of the first tailor shop he found. Despite the notice that the store would not be open that day due to the funeral, he kept on pounding his fist against the hard wood. After ten minutes, a grumpy, silver-haired man who was a tad over half of Laurence's height flung open the door.

The tailor snapped in a clipped tone. "What do you want?"

"I need some clothes for a lady."

"Can't you read? We are closed!"

Laurence pushed past the tailor and entered his store. "I am willing to pay for this mild inconvenience." He reached into the inner pocket of his coat and pulled out a coin purse. He threw it onto the counter, making the gold inside clink. "Will this much do?"

The tailor's attitude changed in an instant. He rubbed his hands together and grinned. "Welcome to our humble store, my good sir. What kind of clothes are you looking for?"

"Hmm. I need a couple of dresses for a noble lady. Something that's already pre-made will do."

Tutting in disapproval, the tailor walked behind the counter. "If you wish to woo the lady, you must put in some effort."

Laurence grimaced. "There is no way I would court that wench." He glared at the tailor. "*Any* dress will do."

"I-I understand. Do you have the lady's measurements, so I could quickly modify the clothes to fit her?"

Rubbing his chin, Laurence tried to recall what Lady Diane looked like at the previous ball they had attended at the imperial palace. "She has a flat chest and her waist is about—" He used his hands to indicate a twenty-eight to thirty inches waistline. "—this big, I think."

The tailor's cheeks flushed red as his thinning brows furrowed. "Is there a particular colour she likes? What about embroidery?"

"Does not matter."

"And is this for everyday use or a formal event?"

"I have no idea. Both?"

The tailor huffed and puffed as he slammed his palms against the counter. "My good sir, are you telling me to find pre-made dresses for a noble whose measurements you are unsure of and with no preferences or knowledge of whether the lady will attend any social gatherings?"

"It doesn't matter. She will be staying at the palace."

The tailor's mouth was agape. He shut it and then opened it again, but no sound came out. With unintelligible grumbling under his breath, the tailor picked up the coin purse and threw it at Laurence, who caught it mid-air. "Does not matter? Are you in your right mind? How can I tarnish the name of my store by providing such a subpar product with no useful information? I will become a laughingstock of the town. No. The whole kingdom!" Sucking in a deep breath, he stormed over to Laurence and pushed him towards the door. "Get out! Get out and do not come back!"

"But I need those dresses!"

"Leave my store immediately before I call the city guards."

Laurence refrained from saying he was one of the royal guards, albeit temporarily. The door behind him slammed shut, making Laurence's ears ring.

He sighed and rubbed his face. He desperately wanted a good night's sleep instead of running errands for His Highness.

Out of the corner of his eye, he saw a familiar boy walking across the street with a dark-haired woman. "Rime?"

The boy's head whipped around in Laurence's direction. "Mornin', Sir Laurel. What brings you 'ere this early?"

"I—" Telling them about the fiasco at the tailor's would make Laurence look foolish. "I came to do some shopping."

"It's an expensive part o' town. What're you lookin' for?" Rime asked, eyeing Laurence's noble attire.

"I need some dresses for a lady."

The woman next to Rime asked in a honeyed voice, "Is it for your sister or your lover?"

Laurence frowned as a sense of familiarity rang bells in his head when he looked at the woman's face. It had a mixture of feminine and masculine features and too much makeup for her to be a noble's daughter. No. She could not possibly be a noble. After all, no lady would ever be seen without an escort, not to mention with a child from the streets. "An acquaintance."

"Are you looking for custom-made items only?" the woman asked.

"You're prying t'much, Ernesto."

Ernesto? Laurence raised a brow at the name. As his eyes focused on the woman's neck, he spotted an Adam's apple there and paled.

A cross-dresser?

"I told you not to use that name when we are out and about!" Ernesto grumbled in a completely masculine voice.

Laurence rubbed his eyes as he tried to wrap his tired brain around the situation. "This may be rude to ask but are you a man?"

"Yes, what of it?" Ernesto's ladylike demeanour was completely gone. Even his posture changed to that of a young man preparing for a street fight.

"See? You scared 'im. Sally told us not'ta scare away the clients!" Rime chided.

Laurence let out an exasperated sigh. "Would you happen to know where I can get some clothes in a hurry for an average girl with a horrid personality?"

Ernesto's brows shot up. "You are quite straightforward."

"I need to get this over with quickly."

Rime nudged Ernesto's side with his elbow. "Just give 'im some o' your old stuff."

"Would the lady mind wearing hand-me-downs?" Ernesto inquired.

Laurence smirked. "I won't tell her if you won't."

With a nod, Ernesto added, "Come with us to the guild."

"As payment," Rime called over his shoulder as he ran ahead, "you've t'buy us some snacks!"

"Not a problem." Laurence laughed. "Pick whatever you want."

The trip to the guild took a lot less time after Rime showed Laurence a shortcut through the back streets. Although the people hidden in the darkest parts of the alleyways looked like unsavoury characters, each one of them smiled at Rime and greeted the boy as if they were all part of a family. That sight made Laurence miss his siblings who had been stationed in different parts of the Hellion Empire. He hardly got to see his brothers in the past ten years. His father, too, became quite involved in imperial politics in recent years, leaving the march's management to Laurence's mother.

Ernesto led the way through the empty halls of the guild house to the second floor where his room was located.

Laurence couldn't help but comment, "Where is everyone?"

"Working," Ernesto replied matter-of-factly.

Rime joined the conversation. "They're helpin' out Lady Em."

The Queen?

Ernesto wagged his finger at the boy. "You shouldn't disclose information like that or Sally'll pull your ears off."

"It's fine. Sir Laurel bought me sweets. He can't be a bad man."

Ernesto smacked Rime on the back of the head. "That's even worse."

Laurence cleared his throat to stop their bickering. "I work for Lady Em, so there is nothing to worry about."

"I know." Ernesto moved away from Rime and went over to a wooden chest that was against the wall. "I saw you at the castle when she got hurt."

"Then there's no need to—"

Ernesto paused in the middle of opening a storage chest and shot a fiery look over his shoulder. "Being close to her doesn't mean you are on her side. The palace is a pit of snakes. She is wounded and even now can only place her faith in outsiders like us to help her. Would you say that is because of the great trust she has in people like you?"

Laurence had no words to defend him. After all, he was there only on Prince Thessian's orders. He would leave Emilia's side in the blink of an eye if His Highness commanded it. He was no better than the royal guards who took the job solely for the fancy title or prestige it got them.

"Look at that, Rime." Ernesto pointed at Laurence. "That is a man whose words hold no water. Just because he bought you sweets, and seems like a decent man, doesn't mean he is worth trusting." Having selected three pastel-coloured dresses, Ernesto threw them into Laurence's arms. "Take these and leave."

Laurence bundled the clothes into a messy ball. "Thank you."

Rime lowered his head and peeked at Laurence from under his brow. "Will you come again, Sir Laurel?"

Laurence winked at the boy. "Sure. Next time, I'll bring you cake."

Ernesto groaned while Rime punched the air and squealed in excitement.

Laurence did not realise how strong Emilia's bond was with the Lionhart Guild. The people working there seemed like they wanted to protect her. Maybe choosing her as regent was not such a bad idea.

Laurence returned to the castle and knocked on the door of the guest room where Lady Diane was staying. When no reply came, he unlocked the door with a spare key the head butler gave him and walked in with a pile of dresses under one arm. He scanned the room, seeing her laying on the bed. Judging by her rapid breathing, she was pretending to be asleep.

He dropped the clothes onto a nearby seat and made his way out of the room when she called out in a trembling voice, "Sir Laurence, is that you?"

Laurence rolled his eyes. She was a terrible actress. Even the ladies in the imperial palace had better mastery of deceit than this fox cub. "What is it, Lady Diane?"

She scrambled off the bed in her dishevelled dress. Landing on her knees before him, she clung to his leg. "Please, Sir Laurence, you must help me! Prince Thessian has lost his mind!"

Fine, I will play along.

He went down on one knee and peeled her hands away. Holding her manicured nails a safe distance away from his face, he gazed at her, full of concern. "My word, Lady Diane! What do you mean by that?"

"He—" She sniffled for effect as she shed a couple of crocodile tears. "He killed my father and his men! Now, he is keeping me captive in this atrocious place as if I am some lowly peasant! I implore you, my good knight, you must help me..."

Laurence briefly scanned the guest room. The furnishings probably cost enough to cover a small town's taxes for a year. "If you were treated as such, would you not be kept in a dungeon?"

She blinked slowly as if processing his words. Then, she returned to her damsel act. "Although the room is...nice, I am kept here against my will. As a knight of the Empire, you must release me and report this to His Imperial Majesty. I promise you, Sir Laurence, you will be handsomely rewarded."

Standing up, Laurence put some distance between them. "But we are not in the Empire, Lady Diane, nor do I serve the emperor. I have sworn my loyalty to one man, and my sword belongs to Prince Thessian alone."

Her tears stopped, and her face turned a deep shade of red. Diane balled her hands against the skirts of her dress. "Shouldn't you be a lady pleaser like the rumours said?"

Laurence laughed. "I only please ladies I like. As for you, I would not even spit in your direction."

"You insolent bastard!" She ran over to a vase as Laurence made his speedy escape. Once he shut and locked the room, multiple objects smashed against the door.

"Harpy," he muttered, shaking his head.

Just the thought of someone like her becoming Prince Thessian's future duchess made Laurence shudder.

20
A GRANDE SECRET

EMILIA

Running on three hours of sleep, Emilia was drowsy when a flurry of maids rushed into her bedchambers first thing in the morning.

Sir Rowell had pulled Ambrose out of the room while Emilia's body was poked, prodded, and stripped naked. A dress she had not seen before was brought in and adjusted to her body on the spot. She put up with some careless pricks of the needles for that. Her long raven hair was tugged and reshaped into different hairstyles until the maids sang praises of Emilia's beauty, which fell on deaf ears. It was as if they had forgotten that it was the funeral of their beloved king and not a coming-of-age ceremony.

At some point, she ended up in front of a full-length mirror with a handful of maids holding expensive jewels on crimson pillows.

"This one matches Her Majesty's eyes best!" the blonde maid

said, lifting an unnaturally bulky sapphire and silver necklace to Emilia's pale neck. At least, the black dress covered Emilia's shoulders, which hid her bandages.

"Well, these earrings match her slender neck better," a chubby brunette with a mole under her eye replied.

Emilia raised her hand, stopping their nattering. "I am not going to wear any jewellery."

The maids seemed so shocked that their mouths didn't want to close.

"Today is my father's and brothers' funeral. Are you trying to imply I should be celebrating their passing?" Emilia also did not think the citizens would appreciate her dressing up in expensive gems and jewels when most of them had to count every copper coin they had.

"No, Your Majesty," they replied in unison, putting the jewellery back.

"Will you be escorted by that handsome man who came here last night?" the blonde dared to ask.

"You dare speak such nonsense?" Emilia met the girl's eyes in the reflection of the mirror, and the maid immediately lowered her head.

Turning around, Emilia clenched her jaw as she raised her head high. The maids did not take her seriously. They had forgotten their lives were spared by Emilia not even four days ago. Yet, they felt so comfortable that they were willing to gossip about her directly to her face.

"What is the head maid doing to be hiring such useless help?" Emilia barked an order at the rest of the maids. "All of you, get out! Bring the head maid here immediately!" She glared at the blonde next. "And you, what is your name?"

With the maid's head bowed low, she stumbled over her words. "M-my na-name is—"

Emilia smirked. "Never mind. I do not need to know the name of someone who will be flogged 'til dawn."

The blonde fell to her knees. "I did not mean t-to offend Your Majesty. It's just, everyone is talking about it…"

"And you thought yourself brave enough to ask me such an impudent question?"

"I have made a grave mistake, Your Majesty. P-please be merciful and s-spare me!"

Emilia crossed her arms with much effort. Her shoulder wound burned like she was stabbed in it all over again. She tolerated the pain and did not let it show on her face. "Since we are on the topic of what others say, what is it the servants have been blabbering about?"

"I would not dare repeat it."

"Oh, repeat it you shall—" Emilia's voice grew colder, "—or your corpse will be buried alongside my family today."

"Please, no!" The maid began to weep as her forehead hit the floor. "They say Her Majesty will bring ruin to this kingdom as the Church of Holy Light has prophesied and that Her Majesty is not the king's real daughter."

Emilia was not surprised that the church had begun to make their move before her official coronation, but the rumours about her being fake? What kind of nonsense was that?

Did Duke Malette's men spread that around?

No matter, Emilia needed someone to keep her in the loop of the rumours. Who best than the terrified girl who wanted to cling to her life?

"Lift your head, girl."

The maid reluctantly raised her head off the floor. There was a harsh red mark on her forehead from pressing it against the floorboards for so long.

"If you do not wish to die, you will serve as my eyes and ears from this day forth. Should word of this get out, I'll have you beheaded and your whole family punished for treason," Emilia commanded.

The blonde's face turned ashen. She shook from head to toe like a leaf, and Emilia wondered if she was going to piss her undergarments next. "I-I will do a-anything for you, Your Majesty!"

Satisfied, Emilia returned to pretending to assess her attire in the mirror. "What is your name?"

"It is G-Galia Every."

"From now on, you will report everything you hear to Ambrose. Should you leave anything out, you know what will happen."

"Y-yes!"

A short while later, the old crone, Head Maid Tamara Hester, along with her flock, arrived with their skirts raised almost to their knees. They must have scampered there from whatever parlour they were playing games in.

Tamara was the one person Emilia hated most among the palace staff. That witch had family ties to a high-ranking noble house in Dante and used her connections to get to her position. From there, she acted high and mighty, especially with Emilia when she was locked away. Today, Tamara's petty reign would come to an end.

"You called for me, Your Majesty?" Tamara asked without lowering her gaze in respect.

Emilia pointed at the floor. "Kneel. All of you."

Tamara cracked a smile. "Your Majesty, surely you are not serious."

"I said *kneel*," Emilia snapped. "Or should I ask the guards to make you?"

Begrudgingly, Tamara lowered her round frame. The other maids quickly complied.

"This maid here, hired by you," Emilia began in a cold tone similar to the one she had to put up with from her father, "has been openly gossiping about a royal. How are you going to atone for your poor teachings?"

"I will educate her properly," Tamara replied eagerly.

"Did you not hear me? I asked how are *you* going to atone for *your* mistake?"

Tamara's wrinkles seemed to deepen all over her saggy face as her brows rose. "You cannot mean—"

"You will be removed from your position immediately. My personal maid, Ambrose, will take your place as the new head maid."

"This is absurd!" Tamara screeched. Her voice alerted the

guards outside the room, and they burst in. One of them was Cali.

Emilia nodded to her knights. "Escort Lady Hester to gather her belongings and off the palace grounds."

"Yes, Your Majesty." Cali caught Tamara by the arm and dragged her out of the room, kicking and screaming. For a noble in her late fifties, Tamara certainly had a lot of energy.

Emilia clapped twice, gathering the attention of the stumped maids. "I believe we were going to select my shoes next."

The maids finally showed Emilia the respect she deserved by acting as they should.

The preparations were completed an hour later, and Emilia had her food served to her office while she read over the recent reports.

Sir Rowell turned up with her tea. As he served it, his right hand trembled enough to make the cup clatter against the saucer.

Emilia lifted her eyes from the report and saw a bandage tightly wrapped around his right hand. "How did you get hurt?"

"This is nothing, Your Majesty. You must give all of your attention to the funeral as you will be leaving the palace soon. Dame Cali should be arriving shortly to escort you to your carriage."

Emilia rubbed her forehead as she blew out a sigh. "I am in a foul mood today, Sir Rowell. Tell me what happened."

"I was stabbed with a fork by the young lady who is kept in the guest room."

Emilia stared at him in disbelief. *The girl Thessian dragged to the palace in the middle of the night dared to harm my servant?*

She erupted from her seat. "Lead the way to her room immediately."

"You really should rest before your departure, Your Majesty."

A stern look from her reminded him of her previous statement.

The butler inclined his head. He guided her through the palace to a locked guest room.

"Open it," she ordered.

The butler used a brass key to undo the lock and opened the door for Emilia.

Emilia's mood turned for the worse when she saw Lady Diane

sitting leisurely on the bed with a forkful of a cream dessert on its way into her wide-open mouth. Striding farther into the room, Emilia stared down the girl.

Sir Rowell rushed to Lady Diane and urged her off the bed. "Lower your head, child, and greet Her Majesty!"

"Why should I?" Lady Diane grumbled. "How can this child be the queen? Prince Thessian is no fool. He wouldn't let someone like her live. Wasn't she supposed to die with the rest of Dante's royalty? I bet this is a puppet he set—"

Emilia wasted no time. She slapped Lady Diane across the face hard enough to leave her palm imprint on the noble's fair skin. "You are here only because Prince Thessian requested I take care of you. Know that I will not tolerate such insults directed towards me or my family."

Clutching her face, Lady Diane glowered at Emilia. Tears reddened her eyes as she bit her lower lip. "You dare hit me?"

"That was for insulting me." Emilia raised her hand and slapped her other cheek. "This is for my servants. Should I hear one more word of you acting out and hurting my people, I will send you straight to a whorehouse where they can make good use of a lady such as yourself."

Fear filled the lady's round eyes, and she shrunk away. Women on the continent wanted to protect their purity more than anything. It was the best card to play to make Diane submit for a short while.

Emilia pressed, "Did you hear me?"

"I did, *Your Majesty*."

Whipping around, Emilia glided out of the room with as much grace as she could muster to not ruin her updo. She didn't want to submit to another two hours of torment in front of a mirror.

She heard Sir Rowell locking the door and catching up to her in the hallway.

"Your Majesty, how is your hand?"

As if on cue, she felt the stinging spreading across her palm. "I will live. Sir Rowell, do not let that harlot take another swing at you. Bring a guard if you cannot handle her alone and make sure to visit the royal physician."

"Thank you for your consideration."

It was barely nine in the morning, and Emilia felt like the day was already too long.

Cali showed up around the corner and blew out a heaving breath. "There you are, Your Majesty! I've been looking everywhere for you. Could you please come with me? There is someone who wishes to meet you."

Whatever made Cali run around the palace had to be urgent. Emilia was sure she still had at least half an hour before she had to climb into a carriage and follow the parade to the blasted Church of the Holy Light.

Is it the prince? "Sir Rowell, return to your duties. Cali, lead the way."

Cali smiled nervously. "Thank you for understanding, Your Majesty."

Emilia cursed under her breath as the trek to their destination was taking about ten minutes. They had climbed one of the towers that belonged to the researcher her father kept around. Emilia never found any of that information interesting because the man disappeared some years ago, and no one had heard from him since. Whatever he was researching had to be useless as King Gilebert did not bother to send out a search party or post wanted posters around the city.

At the top of the tower, the heavy metal door was held open with a rotten crate. Inside the messy room full of dusty round vials and leather-bound tomes stood Prince Thessian with a deep-set scowl on his face as he flicked through the pages of an old notebook.

Cali did not enter, which Emilia found to be odd.

"This is not the best time for a tête-à-tête, Your Highness." Emilia tried to lighten the mood.

Snapping the notebook shut, Thessian demanded, "Did you know Julio Grande was here?"

"Who?" Emilia tilted her head to one side. "Is that the name of the researcher my father kept?"

"That monster is a war criminal from the Hellion Empire," Thessian retorted, his voice rising along with the tension in his body.

Sensing danger, Emilia took a step back. She had no idea who Julio Grande was or how he was related to the Empire. That name was never mentioned in the original story. But then, how much had she changed the original plot by interacting with the characters the real Emilia was never meant to meet?

Are the characters once considered unimportant becoming important?

She thought back to the original storyline. Marquess Walden took hold of the Dante Kingdom soon after the coup, which allowed Prince Thessian to return to his duchy in Darkgate. He never stayed long enough to loiter around and search the towers of the castle.

Is that part of the original plot that was never revealed to the readers or is the world I'm in beginning to create new paths?

Thessian balled his hands into fists. "Do you know where he is?"

Emilia swallowed the knot that was forming in her throat. The prince was a much bigger man than her. If he wanted to end her, she wouldn't be able to escape.

She opted for honesty. "He abandoned his research years ago. I never paid much attention to this as I was a child at the time."

He seemed to cool off after hearing her words. "I apologise. I may have overreacted."

No kidding! I thought I'd pee my pants.

Emilia managed a tiny smile. "Apology accepted."

Thessian ran his hand through his mane of golden hair. "I originally came by to check on Lady Diane and to wish you luck. I heard you would be giving a speech to the nobles later."

She cringed. "Yes. I even brought a handkerchief for the emotional part with fake tears."

He chuckled. "I will try my best to sneak a peek."

Emilia hid her blush by picking up a dusty book off the nearby shelf and flicking through it. The dancing dust in the air made her sneeze. "What is so special about Julio Grande?"

Whether intentionally or not, Cali knocked on the open door. "Your Majesty, we should be getting back."

Emilia spared one last glance at the prince as she placed the book back in its place. "I hope to see you later, Your Highness."

Many possibilities raced through her mind. Without realising it, she managed to get into the carriage and had the knights on horseback guarding her left and right. The sound of trumpets playing her kingdom's hymn reminded her once again of her position. She had an entire nation's future resting on her shoulders.

Unlike in the original story, she hoped Dante Kingdom would not be ravaged by civil war. To protect the livelihoods of people like Ambrose and her sister, her friends at the Lionhart Guild, and even the handful of nobles who weren't greedy pigs. She had to play her part and get the nation stabilised before handing the kingdom to Thessian. By then, hopefully, he would be crowned emperor, and she could retire with Ambrose to the safety of the countryside.

Maybe she would extend the offer to Lionhart and Sir Rowell. They looked like they needed a break, too.

21
MORE QUESTIONS THAN ANSWERS

THESSIAN

When Emilia was gone, Thessian could no longer hold back and punched a wall. All this time, Julio Grande was hiding in Dante after escaping from the Empire. That sick individual deserved to have his head cut off yet remained free from persecution.

Did King Gilebert have a hand in Julio's escape?

He cursed as dull pain spread through his bones. His knuckles had been skinned, but he did not care. The nightmare he witnessed first-hand was hard to forget. All those orphaned children—dead and discarded as if they were no better than yesterday's waste. Thessian was lucky enough to save Ronne and Renne from becoming Julio's next victims.

How much did they remember of what happened six years ago?

Initially, their mental scars were so severe, they acted like living dolls. They needed to be fed, washed, and clothed. Even their eyes did not react to their surroundings. Only after months in Thessian's camp did they begin to show interest in others. To prove their usefulness, the children begged Thessian to give them tasks. As much as it hurt him to do it, he asked them to gather information on the enemy. To his surprise, they did a great job.

Thessian did not regret meeting them. They were more like his younger siblings than Kyros, who remained emotionally unavailable no matter how hard Thessian reached out.

Shaking away useless thoughts, he scanned the room for any additional hints of recent activity. The maids in the castle mentioned they had heard sounds coming from that tower at night, believing it was the ghost of King Gilebert roaming the halls.

Someone was looking for something here. Did Julio forget an item of importance and return for it?

Upon closer inspection, there were deep scrapes in the floorboards that were next to a bookcase.

It had been moved.

Pressing his shoulder against the side of the bookcase, he used his strength to push it away. Behind it was a single door without a handle.

Thessian listened for any movement on the other side.

Silence.

He drew his sword just in case. Since the owner of the room did not want others to come in and took the handle with him, Thessian used his heavy boot to open a path. The door burst off the hinges from the force he applied and banged against the dusty floor.

A small office, a desk, and a handful of loose parchments with what seemed to be Julio's original research could be seen inside. Mana Activation research was forbidden in the Hellion Empire since Thessian reported the atrocities done by Julio and his assistants in the name of science. The nobles who funded the research were sentenced to death by the emperor. The assistants who were caught got beheaded on the spot. All traces of that foul knowledge were kept locked away in the Empire's vault.

Father should have burned those records instead.

Julio must have returned to the tower in recent days while the castle was in disarray. Thessian was certain of it. He would not mistake the strong smell of arnica flowers for anything else. Just like in the previous laboratory belonging to Julio, everything had the same stench from the herbal medicine Julio applied to his weak knee joints. That could only mean one thing. Julio never left Newburn. Instead, he was waiting for an opportunity.

Did King Gilebert throw Julio out for some reason?

Thessian was perplexed as to why King Gilebert would risk harbouring a man wanted by the Empire.

What kind of information did that madman acquire to get safe passage?

Clutching one of the pages with Julio's handwriting on it, Thessian felt his heart racing. This could be a chance to capture him and get the justice Renne and Ronne deserved.

Now, more than ever, Thessian needed to find information before that slippery man escaped for good, and he knew just the place to get it.

22

AN EVENTFUL FUNERAL

EMILIA

The mood on the streets was similar to a festival. The people who came to watch the funeral parade brought their kids, who watched the procession with awe. Food stalls had been set up, and people eagerly queued to get their share of snacks.

Two days ago, Emilia had signed an order to feed the poor and homeless at her expense during the event. That way, some good could come from the death of her family.

From the carriage, she could hear the not-so-subtle murmurings of the crowd.

"Isn't she cursed?" someone asked.

"The priest told me she'll bring calamity to this kingdom."

"D'ya think she's as ugly as the rumours say?"

"What will happen to our kingdom?"

"Will her curse spread to us?"

Emilia gripped the material of her dress in her lap. She kept her eyes trained on her gloved hands as she fought back the tears. Hearing what people thought of her was enough to sink her heart. Just because some church officials determined she would be a perfect scapegoat to instil fear in the hearts of the people, the commoners believed it without question.

A rock smashed through her carriage window, and she covered her head with her hands. The shards managed to miss her exposed skin and scattered around her feet and the seat next to her.

"Your Majesty, are you hurt?" Dame Cali shouted from the outside. "I have dispatched men to catch the culprit!"

So, this is the sentiment I get after being trapped in a tower my whole life? I can't let the church win!

Emilia called back, "I am fine. Please continue on our way."

They had another half of the way to go before arriving at the Church of the Holy Light, which looked like one of those ancient temples in her previous world that had too much money to spare.

The bishop, who hurried to Newburn specifically for the king's funeral, would be leading the sermon. He must have pulled some strings to arrive that fast.

Almost as if he was expecting the deaths...

Through the curtains, Emilia noticed her carriage being rushed to a safer section of Main Street while onlookers were kept at bay by the knights.

After the horses stopped, Sir Laurence opened the door, dressed entirely in Dante's royal guard uniform. Had she not been so shocked by what transpired, she may have commented on how well it suited him.

The concern on his face was hard to miss. "Your Majesty, you look a tad pale."

"I will be fine once this ordeal is over."

"Should we skip the theatrics and hurry to the temple?"

She shook her head. That was exactly what those priests wanted her to do—show weakness they could exploit later. "Sir Laurence, get everyone back on track."

Cries of children followed by demands to see the queen came

from the outside.

Emilia started to move towards the door when Sir Laurence raised his hand to stop her.

"It is too dangerous for Your Majesty to leave the carriage."

She peeled back the curtain and saw a sizeable group of men holding children hostage, blocking the path to the temple. Knives and swords were held against the throats of those helpless children. The crowd for the parade seemed eager to see what was happening and tried to push past the soldiers.

Her knights had surrounded the disruptors. Their swords were drawn and at the ready.

"Sir Laurence, please get out of my way."

He clenched his jaw tight. "I advise against this. This is an obvious trap. The children could be part of the plot to hurt you."

Emilia knew full well that it was a ploy to get her out of the carriage, but she could not hide behind her knights forever. "I remember Sir Laurence boasting he took on two hundred men with His Highness. I feel assured about my safety with you by my side."

"Your Majesty, this is not the time for jests."

"Who said I was jesting? My life is in your hands, Sir Laurence. Now *move*. Do not let me repeat myself."

He stepped aside, offering his hand to help her descend the raised steps onto the cobbled road.

The sun blinded her for a moment after being in the carriage for almost an hour. She straightened her back and lifted her head high.

The citizens who struggled against her guards seemed stumped when they saw her.

Emilia took measured strides towards the armed men. She peeked left and right, noting that they were surrounded by storefronts and houses with guarded alleyways in between. The bandits before her were willing to sacrifice their lives for whatever cause they served.

"Who are you?" Emilia called out, coming to a stop a safe distance away.

Sir Laurence and Dame Cali were right behind her with their hands on the hilts of their swords.

The stout man in a commoner's attire at the forefront of the group, who held on to a young boy no older than eight, said, "Cursed Princess of Dante, Bringer of Destruction, today you will die for your sins!"

Emilia raised a brow. *This church fanatic is probably the leader.* "And what sins would those be?"

He glared at her. "You have been implanting evil thoughts in the minds of children!"

She narrowed her eyes. Thinking back, she did remember seeing those kids at the orphanage she sponsored. How did that information get leaked?

Doing her best, she contained her bubbling anger and kept her voice level. "Would those children be the ones you are currently tormenting?"

"Tormenting?" He scoffed. "They are nothing more than demons shaped in your image!" His frustration caused the blade of his sword to dig into the boy's skin. A tiny river of blood ran down the child's small neck.

The boy sobbed harder as did the rest of the children involved.

Their cries tore at Emilia's heart. She wanted to throw the dagger strapped to her ankle at the culprit's head but that would not resolve the situation. Instead, such an act could endanger the children further.

Apparently, it was her fault for asking the nuns to teach the children reading and writing. When she was visiting Ambrose and Ivy, she often brought books for the other children to read.

Is that what he's referring to? "What do you want?"

"I already told you." The man's face darkened as he sneered. "Your death."

"Your Majesty, I suggest you withdraw to safety with Sir Laurence," Dame Cali whispered behind Emilia.

Sir Laurence added, "Reasoning with a lunatic will get us nowhere. We will do what we can for the young ones, but your life is more important."

Emilia couldn't tear her eyes away from the frightened eyes on those small faces. They reminded her of her younger self. She was all alone, in a cold tower, with no one to talk to or protect her. Her father thought she was an abomination, and her brothers believed her only value was to entertain them when they were bored. No one helped her or spared a kind word. She was alone in an unknown world with the memories of her previous life that was equally as shitty.

Here and now, she was no longer alone. She was strong enough to defend herself, unlike those kids.

"If you release the children," Emilia said in an authoritative tone, "I will go with you to help ensure your escape. Then, you can do whatever you want with me."

The leader of the group licked his lips. "Come here first!"

"Your Majesty!" Sir Laurence pleaded. "You cannot seriously be considering such a deal."

Emilia muttered to Dame Cali, "Secure the children and bring them to safety when there is an opening."

"I must agree with Commander," Dame Cali replied in desperation. "This is far too dangerous."

Emilia motioned for the knights encircling the bandits to move to one side. She took two more steps forward. "If you release half of the children now, I will come willingly. My guards will remain on standby until you are out of sight."

"Fine." The leader nodded to his men.

Five children were let go and allowed to run to the open arms of the knights.

Emilia sucked in a steadying breath. She had to fulfil her end of the bargain. Maintaining her regal posture, she kept walking to the leader whose eyes were trained on her.

As she was almost in front of him, she smirked. "Do you believe in karma?"

He frowned. "What's that?"

"It is when your evil deeds come back to bite you in the buttocks." She clicked her fingers, and an arrow lodged itself between his thick brows. As expected, Ambrose and Lionhart were on standby the whole time, keeping watch over the event from the rooftops.

The bandits began to panic, some lunging at her with their weapons.

Emilia retrieved her dagger and rammed it into the throat of an attacker coming towards her.

Another arrow pierced the man's neck to her right.

The rest of the bandits were quickly surrounded by her knights and cut down one by one. Seeing Sir Laurence and Dame Cali taking on two or three bandits at a time was a sight to see. Their fluid movements and practised swings made it seem as if they were dancing instead of butchering their enemies.

The funeral parade became a death parade instead.

Emilia wiped her dagger with her handkerchief and dropped it next to a dead body. Over her shoulder, she saw the children she saved. They did not look at her with gratitude or reverence. They appeared more terrified of her than of the men who kidnapped them.

She faced her citizens who watched the show with interest and occasional cheers.

"Citizens of Newburn," Emilia addressed them loud enough to gain their attention. "As you can see, I am not an ugly monster nor am I cursed. As your Queen, my only wish is to bring prosperity, ease your suffering, and help those in need. As of this day, I wish to make it clear to everyone here. I do not care if you are a noble or a commoner. If you have skills or ideas that would benefit our homeland, come to the palace and serve the kingdom. That is all."

She returned to her carriage and slumped in her seat.

That was nerve-wracking. Thank God, I didn't stumble and fall on my face!

Sir Laurence arrived in the doorway of her carriage shortly after. His voice trembled with anger. "Dame Cali sent the children back to the orphanage with some knights. We should be on our way shortly, Your Majesty."

"You look like you want to say something else."

"Of course! How could you do something so dangerous?" He climbed inside and shut the door behind him. "You could have died."

"Yes, and you would have been out of a job."

"This is not funny!"

"I know." Emilia leant forward and took hold of his shaking hand. "Thank you, Sir Laurence, for doing your best to protect me."

His cheeks turned red, and he looked away as the carriage began to move. "Why did you not tell us about the archers?"

"Your calm reaction would alert the enemies."

"I guess you are right." He faced her again, his eyes sparkling with interest. "So, who was it? That first shot was pretty spectacular!"

"It was, wasn't it?"

"Are you not going to tell me?"

"A lady must keep her secrets."

Emilia smiled as Sir Laurence released more complaints. His deep voice managed to drown out the harsh and bitter comments of the people who still believed her to be a monster.

Finally, the carriage stopped at the foot of the temple that stood on a snowy hill. Long white steps led to huge stone pillars that reached towards the sky. Getting out of the carriage with the help of Sir Laurence, Emilia felt like an ant. Even the palace did not make her feel so small.

How could the Church of the Holy Light afford to construct such a monstrosity? Just how many of Dante's nobles were siding with His Holy Pompousness?

A stony-faced bishop descended the steps with a flock of priests at his heel, all dressed in white robes with golden embroidery on their stoles. The bishop's hat reminded Emilia of an ice cream cone with two scoops. She converted her chuckle into a light cough.

"Greetings, Your Majesty. May the blessings of Luminos guide you," the bishop said with a strained smile. "You are late. Did something happen?"

After the day Emilia had, she was ready to punch a priest, dig her father's grave with her own hands, and give the church her middle finger. Not like they would understand the meaning of the latter. In her new world, gesticulating in insult depended on the kingdom. Among Dante's common folk, all she had to do was lick her palm and then slap her knee to insult a person. She kept asking Lionhart and Sally for the meaning behind it, but they avoided the answer.

"May the blessings of Luminos guide you, Bishop Lagarde." *The bishop was probably the one behind the attack earlier.* Emilia smiled back. "Let us get on with the mass. I am sure the nobles gathered at the temple are eager to hear your teachings."

Lagarde blocked her way when she started for the steps. "As I recall, Her Majesty was never baptised in the Church of the Holy Light. I am sorry, but you cannot enter the temple without your soul being blessed by our Lord."

I mustn't punch a priest. I mustn't punch a priest.

She smiled as she tilted her head towards the sunny skies and recited the church's baptismal rights on the spot. It took her five minutes to get through the entire ritual. It wasn't easy to get her hands on the text. Good thing Lionhart was a resourceful man who *borrowed* a sacred book from the temple for her that one time.

When she finished, the dumbfounded look on the bishop's face was worthy of being captured in a painting and hung in her office. "Please, bless me, Bishop Lagarde. I believe that is all that is left to do aside from splashing some holy water on me. I assume a holy man such as yourself has some on you, yes?"

He ground his teeth as he reached into his inner pocket and pulled out a silver flask with the crest of the church on it. Spraying some onto his palm, he sprinkled the holy water around Emilia in a dramatic fashion. Then, he lifted his left palm over her head. "From now on, may this child serve our Lord, God of Light, and be cleansed of her previous sins."

"Now can we get on with the mass?" she asked sweetly.

The bishop whipped around and scaled the steps. The rest of the priests rushed ahead to the carriage with the coffins.

When entering the temple, Emilia could see why they called it the 'Church of the Holy Light'. Golden streams of light descended from the dome-like, glass roof onto the nave. The rest of the vaulted ceilings were equally as breathtaking with a mixture of rare redwood and clear white marble. Tall statues of Luminos and his semi-naked angels lined the aisles to the chancel.

Emilia took her seat in the first row. The row behind her was empty while the rest of the pews were filled with noblemen and women clad in black.

Sir Laurence and Dame Cali stood off to one side, their eyes assessing the room for any threats.

The second the bishop opened his mouth to speak, Emilia zoned out. The mass was the same no matter whether it was in her old world or the fantasy novel she ended up in. For the majority of the service, she tried her best not to doze off.

Who knew if the bishop would attempt to kill her again and claim she was struck down by Luminos through his body?

After the mass, the time to give her speech came. Emilia got up to the chancel and faced the nobility from behind the marble podium. As she had a perfect memory, she did not need notes. Somehow, that did not take away from her nervousness.

"May the blessings of Luminos guide you," she began, hoping to score some points with the religious folk. "I wish to thank you for attending this wonderful mass for my dear father and brothers who have lived and fought for the Dante Kingdom. Their lives were short yet full of valiant endeavours, and I, Princess Emilia Valeria Dante, as the sole heir to the throne, will do my best to fulfil my father's ambitions in turning this kingdom into a land of prosperity and knowledge. Please grant me your support in the future and spare a prayer for the souls of my dearest family, who are now by Luminos' side."

Her eyes searched every corner of the church.

In the end, Prince Thessian did not show up.

Nevertheless, the nobles seemed content. They clapped once her speech was over and formed a long line to give her their empty condolences.

QUEEN OF DECEPTION

Eventually, Count Baudelaire's turn arrived.

Lord Baudelaire bowed his head. "My deepest condolences for your loss, Your Majesty." He then lowered his voice. "I have received a report from my soldiers at the palace that Duke Malette has escaped."

She nodded and held his hand, pretending he had said something heartfelt. "Thank you for your kind words. There is no need to worry."

"I am glad to hear that." He withdrew his hand. "Now, if you will excuse me. I will be on my way to say my final goodbye to the late king."

"Yes, of course."

Dame Cali stepped up to Emilia. "Would you like to do the same, Your Majesty?"

"Yes, even if my heart can't bear it, I must say my final goodbyes," she replied as she dabbed at her non-existent tears.

Sniffling, Emilia apologised in a strangled voice to the rest of the nobles who were queuing and left.

When Count Baudelaire was done with his show of respect for the deceased, Emilia picked up one of the lilies next to King Gilebert's coffin. She placed the flower on top of the elder wood and leaned in until her face was an inch away from the glossy lid.

To others, it may have looked like she was crying. In reality, she was whispering curses that had built up over the years in her heart. For effect, she dabbed at the corners of her eyes with the handkerchief she had borrowed from Sir Laurence in the carriage and moved aside for the next person who wanted to pretend as if they had cared about the previous king.

23
RECKLESS

LAURENCE

Laurence sat in the carriage across from Emilia on their way back to the palace. She had her eyes closed. Her breathing was slow and even. That was the first time Laurence had seen her so defenceless. Around him and Prince Thessian, she had not once let her guard down. The maid she kept around often eyed Laurence as if he was a pest.

Crossing his arms, he studied her beautiful face. Her long, dark eyelashes and red lips contrasted against her pale skin. She was petite and eye-catching like a fairy.

What kind of terrible life a young girl like her lead to not trust a single soul?

Today, she must have been truly exhausted. After all, she fell asleep in a man's presence. He shooed the strange thoughts away. Not like he would do anything to a sleeping person. His mission always came first.

Laurence diverted his attention to the passing scenery outside of the window. In all honesty, he thought his hair would turn white when she decided to get close to the kidnappers on the street.

How could she be so reckless?

Not only did she partake in a duel with a guild master where she nearly died, but she was also eager to hop into dangerous situations left and right. She needed a round-the-clock bodyguard.

Folding his arms behind his head, he thought, *I guess, it's not so bad.*

From the corner of his eye, he saw her head lolling to one side. Without thinking, he jolted out of his seat and stood in front of her, holding up her head. The rocking of the carriage made it impossible to stay still, so he slipped into a seat next to her and carefully let her head rest against his shoulder.

A subtle scent of roses wafted from her hair. He turned his face away, feeling his ears burning.

What the hell am I doing? This is merely my duty as a knight. Nothing more.

By the time the carriage came to a stop in front of the palace, Laurence managed to calm himself by naming all the ladies in Hellion court from oldest to youngest.

The door was opened by Cali. She was about to say something when Laurence lifted his hand to stop her.

"No need to be quiet." Emilia covered her yawn with her hand. She sat upright and winked at Laurence. "Your shoulder is not a great cushion, Sir Laurence. Next time, you have my permission to use your thigh."

Cali gasped. "I-I have to give out some orders to the soldiers..." She scurried off.

Hearing such audacious words from Emilia made Laurence's face burn.

Emilia climbed out of the carriage with his help. When her feet touched the ground, she asked, "Are you not going to chase after her? Dame Cali may have taken my joke seriously."

"Cali and I do not have that kind of relationship."

"Very well. Lead the way to my office, Sir Laurence."

He inclined his head and proceeded to escort her. Each silent minute between them made things all the more awkward. What was he thinking by letting her rest against him? No. As a gentleman, he could not let her head fall like that.

She is not any young lady, Laurence. She's a queen. Ugh! What am I going to tell His Highness when he hears about this?

"I can get there by myself if you feel uncomfortable," her comment broke him out of his reverie.

"I am fine. Thank you for your concern." He sped up.

Emilia stopped in her tracks, causing him to pause as well.

"Why did we stop?"

She motioned to the door on her right. "We have arrived, haven't we?"

"Ah, right..." He opened the door for her. "Please rest inside. I will be out here."

"Could you summon Sir Rowell?"

"Of course, Your Majesty." He gave one of his charming smiles and hurried away.

Moving his body allowed him to calm his troubled mind. This was a temporary assignment. Once the situation in Dante stabilised, Laurence would receive a new mission from Thessian and leave that tiny kingdom.

Things will soon return to normal.

Having queried multiple maids, Laurence found Sir Rowell in the kitchen, preparing tea for Emilia. *What a thoughtful butler...*

"Sir Rowell, Her Majesty is looking for you. Although, it seems you were on your way to see her," Laurence commented, picking up an apple from a fruit bowl and biting into it.

Sir Rowell scowled. "Where are your manners? Have you forgotten them in the Hellion Empire?"

"I was hungry after guarding the Queen all day. Fighting bandits can take a lot out of a person, you know."

"Was there an altercation in the city?" He nearly dropped the teapot. "Is Her Majesty safe?"

"Would I be here if she wasn't?"

The head butler regained his composure. He walked past Laurence, skilfully smacking the apple out of Laurence's hand before he could take another bite. "You are not a dog. Eat when it is mealtime."

Laurence glared at the back of the old man's head as he shuffled out of the kitchen. Out of spite, he selected another two apples from the bowl and made off with them.

On his way back to Emilia's office, he bumped into Prince Thessian who was staring blankly at the fountain in the courtyard.

Laurence approached him. "Your Highness, I was not expecting you to be at the castle."

"I went to the Lionhart Guild for information to find no one there. I thought you said they were good."

Laurence let out a nervous laugh. "They are good, Your Highness, but they have been tied up with helping the Queen today."

Thessian finally faced Laurence. "Why did Emilia enlist the help of the guild?"

"Who knows? Maybe she did not trust we could protect her. Well, she was not wrong. Had she not prepared in advance, she may have died."

"And what were you doing the entire time? Do not tell me you have been shirking your duties!"

The anger in the prince's voice startled Laurence. He was used to casually stirring up trouble and avoiding Thessian's outbursts, yet Laurence never directly faced an angry prince.

"What information were you looking for, Your Highness? I thought the deal with Marquess Walden is done."

"This is not about the Marquess. It is about Julio Grande. I found his research station in one of the towers."

Laurence stuck his pinkie in his ear and cleaned it. "Come again? Did you mean the swine who did all those horrible things to Renne and Ronne?"

"The very same."

Laurence gritted his teeth. "Does Emilia know?"

"I have already spoken with her. She knew nothing of it."

"She is too smart not to take notice of someone like that," Laurence countered. "What if she is involved somehow?"

"Enough, Laurence." Thessian patted his subordinate on the shoulder. "I believe Emilia. She had nothing to do with Julio's presence here." He stepped back and crossed his arms. "We both want to catch Julio and bring him to justice, which is why I ordered Cali to search the castle while we check the city."

"The parade is over, so the guild members should be done with their tasks," Laurence commented. "They may know something."

"We will visit them together. If we are still unsuccessful, we may need to bring more men into the city."

"That would cause quite a commotion, Your Highness. The queen's position could be in danger if the nobles who are against her suspect she is a pawn."

Thessian looked away as he lowered his arms. "We may have no choice. If worse comes to worst, we will take over by sheer force until they submit."

Laurence pressed his lips into a tight line. Such an outcome would be disastrous as many deaths would follow. With the current scheme, taking over Dante had allowed them to assume control with minimal bloodshed. An all-out war could make for a lot of uncertainty since Marquess Walden had been captured. They could no longer rely on Walden's forces for backup. Their army was split in half because of that. Who knows if the nobles who supported their coup would continue to do so now that Emilia took over?

"Please rethink this, Your Highness."

"I told you, that is the worst possible outcome. Let us focus on finding Julio for the time being."

"Alright."

24

THE LONELY QUEEN

EMILIA

The peppermint tea Sir Rowell brought was what she needed after the hellish day she had. Sitting on the sofa, she inhaled the rejuvenating aroma and glanced at the butler. "Have you completed the preparations?"

"Yes, Your Majesty. Ambrose will be able to assume the position of head maid without any further resistance. Also, Lady Tamara Hester has been expelled from the palace as you have ordered."

"What about the knights? Did any of them do anything suspicious after Duke Malette was captured?"

"I have been keeping an eye on the correspondence going in and out of the palace. I have no solid proof, but the contents of Sir Lucroy's letters were a bit strange."

"How so?"

"They are all pie recipes. As far as I am aware, Sir Lucroy has never cooked in his entire life."

Emilia rubbed her chin. "The recipes probably contain a coded message. Hand them over to Lionhart when he takes on the role of spymaster. Also, inform Dame Cali to keep a close eye on Sir Lucroy's actions from this day forth and note whom he interacts with the most. She should not assign any important tasks to him that could jeopardise the security of my aides."

Sir Rowell placed his hand over his heart and bowed. "I will do as you have instructed, Your Majesty."

"Is there anything else?"

"I must ask, why have you allowed that hooligan, Sir Laurence, to be your guard? I believe he is unworthy of such an important position."

Emilia sipped her tea, enjoying its strong flavour on her tongue. "He is not someone to be underestimated. Sir Laurence managed to keep the position of Prince Thessian's second-in-command for the past seven years. I, too, have witnessed that he can hold his own in a fight. Please, try to tolerate him."

"I will do my best."

A knock on the door was followed by the entrance of Ambrose and Lionhart.

Emilia's mood brightened at the sight of them. "Sir Rowell, please do as instructed."

The head butler excused himself, closing the door behind him.

Lionhart collapsed into the armchair nearby and stretched out his legs in front of him. From her seat, Emilia could see the shiny lightweight alloy of his false leg peeking out from under his trouser leg. "What a day!"

"Tell me about it," Emilia mumbled into her cup.

"We have received news from Mister Jehan Wells about the location of Duke Malette, Your Majesty. He was accompanied by two men dressed as palace guards," Ambrose eagerly informed Emilia. "He is hiding in an abandoned mansion on Sudest Street."

Emilia imagined the pompous Duke Malette putting up with cobwebs and grime and laughed. "He must be having quite a pleasant time, indeed."

"Most definitely, Your Majesty," Ambrose replied.

Lionhart folded his arms over his stomach. "When are you planning to make your move?"

Emilia set her cup aside. "I need to know who else is involved in his escape. The more weeds we can pull out in one go, the cleaner the field will be. Continue to keep an eye on him. When he makes his next move, I will capture him along with his accomplices."

Lionhart nodded. "I will have Jehan and Ernesto keep an eye out."

"I owe you one," Emilia said.

"I am not doing this for free," Lionhart admitted. "You promised to buy enough drink to keep my men drunk for a month. I will hold you to that."

"Yes, I sent the purchase orders last night. The finest of Baudelaire wine should arrive in your warehouse in a fortnight." Looking at her maid, Emilia added, "Get some rest, Ambrose. You have been on your feet all day."

Ambrose's face fell. "I could not possibly rest before you! It is you who has been working hard while wounded. I did what was expected of me."

"Thank you." Emilia meant every word. "And thank you both for saving my life today. I would not have saved those kids if it weren't for your backup."

Lionhart shrugged. "No need to thank me. Ambrose took the first shot."

Emilia's eyes grew wide as she stared at her maid. "You have gotten pretty good!"

Ambrose's cheeks turned bright red. "I am thankful for your praise, Your Majesty."

After he was upright, Lionhart stretched. "Well then, I best return to the guild. I need to catch up on my beauty sleep. I will send a messenger should the situation with the Duke change."

"Wait." Emilia knotted her hands in her lap. "There is something I need you to look into."

Lionhart sat back down and leaned in, resting his elbows on his knees.

Emilia continued, "I need information on someone named Julio Grande. Thessian seems eager to locate him, and I would like to help him if I can."

"Why are you taking on needless tasks?" Lionhart inquired. "You are quite busy as it is."

"According to Thessian, Julio is a war criminal from the Hellion Empire. He has been staying in one of the towers at the palace for almost five years. I doubt he went by the same name if he was in hiding. If this news gets out, it could cause quite a headache for me."

Lionhart scratched his head. "King Gilebert must have lost his mind to let a man like that into his home."

"My father was a greedy man," Emilia explained without any emotion. "Julio probably brought something to the table that the late king wanted."

"I will query my contacts in Hellion about him," Lionhart said, rising. "Stay alert. There are many people after your head."

Emilia waved goodbye, and Ambrose escorted him to the door.

What a long day...

Emilia felt like her shoulders were ready to come off from the weight she carried as a monarch. At least, she didn't need to wear her crown daily. "Ambrose, how are you doing?"

The maid smiled. "I am fine, Your Majesty."

"Tell me if you are feeling unwell or if your workload is too much. I have ordered you to become the head maid to get rid of the useless people around here. Should a maid not wish to serve as my eyes and ears, cut her loose and hire someone else."

"Understood."

"And make use of the maid named Galia Every."

"You have scared her well. She has given me a brief report when I returned to the palace. "

Emilia raised a brow. That was quicker than she had anticipated. In a way, she half-expected Galia to quit and search for work elsewhere. "Anything useful?"

"Not yet."

"I guess it is still too early." Emilia rose from her seat and gently massaged her sore shoulder. The dull pain had been increasing in intensity over the past half an hour. Her painkillers must have stopped working. "Have the physician come by to check on my wound before my bath and then get some rest."

"I can go on without sleep for one more—"

"That is an order, Ambrose. Rest well. I do not need you collapsing from exhaustion."

Ambrose lowered her head. "I apologise for worrying you. I will retire for the night after you fall asleep."

Emilia pinched the bridge of her nose. There was no use in arguing with Ambrose any further. Not like her maid would listen anyway.

"Do as you will." She strode towards the door and paused in front of it. Speaking over her shoulder, she added, "Bring some desserts to my room. Let us celebrate the death of my so-called family."

"Are you sure that will not anger their spirits?"

"I never took you for a superstitious person."

"I sometimes pray for the souls of my parents. They have worked hard to keep Ivy and me alive."

Bitterness surfaced in Emilia's heart. She had never felt parental love. Not in this world nor the previous. The idea that a parent was there to help or protect her was alien to her.

"I will party without you then."

"Your Majesty, I—"

"There is no need for you to be here anymore. Summon Galia to my room and go to bed. Dismissed."

Emilia marched out of her office without looking back.

She knew it was wrong to punish Ambrose for her terrible luck with her parents. Not everyone in the world was like her. As far as she knew, Prince Thessian and Sir Laurence were from whole families. That was the reason why Emilia fit best with the misfits at the Lionhart Guild. They never thought of her as an outsider and treated her as an equal. Even after they discovered she was the 'Cursed Princess', their treatment of her did not change. But Ambrose no longer had a family to rely on. Just like Emilia, she had to grow up early and rely only on herself.

Coming to a halt in the middle of the hallway, she spun around and walked back to her office. There, Ambrose remained in the same spot with her cheeks streaked with tears. A pang of guilt stabbed Emilia's heart.

She used her good arm to envelop Ambrose in a hug. "I am so sorry. I spoke without thinking."

"Am I no longer needed, Your Majesty?" Ambrose clung to Emilia's dress and wept into her shoulder.

From their first meeting at the orphanage, Emilia had never witnessed Ambrose's tears. Her maid had put up a strong front and worked tirelessly to support her younger sister. She trained in archery, hand-to-hand combat, sword fighting, reading, writing, linguistics, herbalism, and politics without protest. Deep down, Emilia envied Ambrose's dedication to her family to the point where she hated herself for doing so.

"There, there." Stroking Ambrose's hair, Emilia murmured in her ear, "You are the only one who is truly on my side, Ambrose. I'd never want to lose you."

Ambrose peeled away from Emilia and wiped her snotty nose with a handkerchief she kept in her pocket. "I will serve you forever, Your Majesty. Please don't discard me."

"I know." Emilia offered Ambrose her hand. "Shall we get some sweets to cheer you up?"

Ambrose finally smiled. "Thank you."

25
A CHILDHOOD LOST

THESSIAN

Thessian stepped inside the Lionhart Guild as night fell over the busy city. The loss of a king and the princes had not changed the mood in the slightest. The people moved on as if nothing of note had happened. That proved his decision to invade Dante was the correct one. With a change in leadership and, eventually, joining the Hellion Empire, Dante Kingdom would be better off.

A female dwarf walked over to him and lifted her head to study Thessian. Although her face was small, her nose was bulbous. She pointedly eyed Laurence. A long brown braid rested on her shoulder, matching the colour of her eyes. "You brought another strange man here, Sir Laurel?"

Laurence covered his chuckle with a cough into his hand. "This is my lord, Miss Sally. He wishes to do business with the guild."

"I would like to meet the guild master," Thessian interjected.

"Like master like servant…" She waved for them to follow. "You can wait for him in his office. He should be back soon."

They scaled the stairs to the top floor.

The attic had been converted into a lavishly decorated office with plush red velvet furniture. Intricate paintings of captivating country scenery decorated the walls and were signed by an artist named K. Cornell. Thessian once heard that name mentioned during a spring ball. He was a sought-after painter who rarely sold his work to others. It was next to impossible to keep him in one place because he was known as a free spirit.

What kind of favour did Lionhart do for Cornell to get so many paintings?

"Have a seat," Sally instructed and made her way to the drinks cabinet. She retrieved a bottle of expensive ale and two silver goblets. Once she arranged everything neatly on a tray, she brought it over to an end table next to a sofa that was crafted well enough to be among the palace furniture. "Here is something to drink. I hope you won't mind waiting."

Laurence folded his arms over his chest and rested his back against the wall. "You are much nicer to my master, Miss Sally."

"He does not seem like a time-waster."

"And I do?" Laurence asked, incredulous.

"Very much so."

Thessian laughed. "You were right, Laurence. This guild must be good."

"I'm pleased you think so, milord," Sally ignored Laurence's complaints and backed away to the door. "I must excuse myself. Some matters need my attention."

Thessian settled in and enjoyed the drink provided. His thoughts kept going back to Emilia. She had to be upset. After all, she had buried her father and siblings mere hours ago. Had he lost his family, he would be devastated.

Should I go see her?

"Your Highness, what are you thinking so hard about?"

Thessian sighed. "I am thinking about getting a gag for your birthday."

"As happy as I am to have you think of me to such an extent, I would rather you give me some time off to find a lady."

"You do not need time off for that. You shamelessly flirt wherever you go."

Laurence gasped. "I would never flirt when I am on duty."

"Tell that to all of the broken-hearted women you've left behind during our campaign."

"In all seriousness—" Laurence dropped the playfulness from his speech, "—are you planning to turn Dante upside down for Julio? He has been in hiding for a long time without anyone noticing. There is a high chance someone else is his backer."

"Someone other than King Gilebert?"

"Yes. We should tread carefully."

The door to the room opened, and a dark-skinned man Thessian barely recognised limped in. Unlike during their first meeting, the guild master had his hair tied back into a ponytail and wore a cream-coloured, knee-length coat. His facial hair had been tidied enough for Thessian to wonder if he was mistaken.

Laurence voiced his thoughts out loud, "Are you the guild master?"

"I am." Lionhart greeted Thessian with a businessman smile as he sat across from the prince. "How may I help you, Prince Thessian of the Hellion Empire? Or should I refer to you by your new title, Duke of Darkgate?"

Thessian studied the man intently a second longer. Where had Lionhart's hostility gone? "You are no longer glaring at me."

"You were not a client before."

Leaning forward in his seat, Thessian reached into his inner pocket and pulled out a heavy coin purse. He tossed it to Lionhart who caught it with ease. "I need you to find the location of a man named Julio Grande. That amount should more than cover a simple search inquiry."

Lionhart threw the coin purse up and down in his hand. "A simple search that all of Hellion Empire's soldiers were unable to complete?"

"You keep well-informed," Thessian stated.

"I do own an information guild." Lionhart handed the money back to Thessian. "You can make the payment when the job is done, but you will no longer be dealing with me." Raising his voice, he called, "Sally!"

The dwarf leisurely entered the room. "Where's the fire, Lionhart?"

"This gentleman will be dealing with you from now on."

Thessian shook his head. "I will only deal with the guild master."

"Starting tomorrow, she will be in charge of this place," Lionhart explained.

Laurence piped in, "Early retirement?"

"I will be taking on a new role at the palace," Lionhart corrected him.

Thessian furrowed his brow. "What role would that be?"

The guild master smirked. "If you want to find out, speak with Her Majesty."

"Then why did you come here?" Thessian pressed, tapping his fingers on the armrest.

"I wanted to know what Your Highness wanted." Lionhart got up and offered his seat to his replacement. "The prince here is searching for a war criminal, Sally. Make sure to charge him extra."

Thessian shot out of his seat and stormed over to Lionhart. Before he could grab him, the guild master easily evaded his hand. "What do you know about Julio? Where is he?"

Adjusting his coat sleeves, Lionhart said, "That is as far as my knowledge goes, Your Highness. The man you are searching for must be using an alias within Dante's territory otherwise he would have been discovered."

Laurence appeared beside Thessian. "Calm down, Your Highness."

Only then had Thessian realised he was clenching his fists so tight, the bones in his hands ached. He sucked in a calming breath. "I apologise. As you can see, this is a sensitive subject."

"Indeed…" Lionhart sat next to Sally. "I think I will stay and listen to your request."

"Very well." Thessian resumed his seat, and Laurence joined him. The ale Sally initially provided seemed like a good idea after the commotion. He downed his drink and wiped his mouth with the back of his hand. "Julio Grande must be caught. He has harmed my subordinates and the people of the Empire. I cannot let a man like that out of my grasp."

Sally was the first to ask, "Do you have a description?"

Thessian thought back to the day when Julio was arrested. "Julio has blond hair, average face for a Hellion man, average height, scrawny. He smells of arnica flowers."

"He is scrawny compared to you, Your Highness," Laurence added.

"Yes, you may be right."

Lionhart buried his face in his palm. "So, the Empire is searching for an average man? As far as I recall, most of the population in Hellion is blond. Are you here to mock us?"

"No!" Thessian countered. "There simply is nothing distinct about him other than his research."

"What kind of research?" Lionhart probed.

Thessian gripped an empty goblet. He hated thinking about Julio's research as much as voicing it out loud. "He wanted to find out if he could forcibly activate and deactivate a mage's power. Most of his victims were orphaned children who were left behind during the war. Before I got to his laboratory, he had killed hundreds of orphans under the age of twelve."

The room fell silent.

Thessian got a chill running down his spine. He found that the ominous feeling of bloodlust came from Lionhart. Just like Thessian, the guild master had certainly taken many lives in his lifetime.

What kind of past was Lionhart hiding?

Sally elbowed Lionhart in the side and cleared her throat loudly. "Our guild will gladly take on this assignment."

Lionhart said nothing. He abruptly stood and muttered a farewell before striding out of the room with a slight limp.

"We will take payment after the job is complete," Sally said.

"Thank you, Miss Sally." Thessian set the goblet aside and rose from his seat. "I believe he may still be in Newburn. If you find anything, please inform me no matter the hour."

"That makes the search much easier," the dwarf added with a warm smile that cheered him up a notch.

With Laurence following, Thessian left the guild. Next to their horses, Ronne was spinning a dagger on his palm.

Upon seeing Thessian, Ronne's posture became stiff as he took on his military stance. "I came here to report, Your High—"

Laurence clasped his hand over the young man's mouth. "Shh! This is not our camp. Act as you would around your friends."

Ronne mumbled something into Laurence's palm and frowned.

Removing his hand, Laurence asked, "What?"

"I don't have any friends, only superiors."

"Then act as you would with your sister."

Ronne grimaced. "What? No! I could never act like that around His Hi—I mean, my lord."

Thessian untied his horse and pulled himself up into the saddle. "Tell me what happened on the way to the camp. We have changed locations since the advance forces arrived."

The others climbed onto their horses, and they rode out of the city. Once they were outside of Newburn's walls, they slowed enough for Thessian to listen to Ronne's report.

"A small force of Duke Malette's men have disguised themselves as workers and entered the city through the sewers." Ronne paused to take a breath. "I have followed them to the southeast part of the city. There, they have met up with another thirty men."

"What could the duke be planning with that many men?" Laurence asked.

"Report this to the Queen in the morning, Laurence. Ronne and I will head to camp."

Laurence groaned. "And here I thought I could finally get some sleep…"

"You can sleep when you are dead," Thessian replied.

"I should have picked a kinder master," Laurence grumbled.

"One who would praise me and give me bonus pay now and then."

Thessian fired a glare at his chatty subordinate. "Are you complaining about your salary? Shall I demote you to a squire?"

"Have I told you how glad I am to serve such a kind and caring master? This humble servant will serve you day and night, so please do not cut my pay! Ronne, back me up here!"

Ronne shrugged. "I am glad to receive whatever wages my lord gives me."

Laurence saluted Thessian. "I will be off to fulfil my duty as your faithful yet slightly underpaid servant." He galloped away before Thessian could swing a punch.

"Ronne, you must never use Laurence as your role model," Thessian told the fifteen-year-old scout.

"Sir Laurence is quite spoiled by you."

"I agree. Maybe I should cut his pay, after all."

Unlike Renne who sometimes smiled, Ronne hardly ever showed a happy expression. Thessian wanted to spoil the twins but knew that preferential treatment within his unit would affect morale. They, too, seemed eager to fit in with the rest of the knights by joining in on the gruelling training every day. Because of Julio's rotten experiment, they were robbed of their childhood.

Had that researcher not gotten his hands on them, would they lead happier lives?

Thessian wasn't sure if their stay at a rundown orphanage would have been a much more pleasant experience than becoming part of the military at an extremely young age. At least, he managed to keep the children from killing by giving them predominantly scouting jobs.

26

HOUSE ESCARIOT

EMILIA

Emilia **walked through the dark,** empty halls of her palace. The eerie silence broke from the sound of her nightdress rustling with her steps. In search of her people, she arrived in front of the throne room and pushed open the large doors.

There, glimmering lights from the golden chandeliers enveloped the nobles who were partaking in ballroom dance. They spun in an endless sea of colour, making her dizzy.

As she waded through the ever-moving crowd, she saw Ambrose, Lionhart, and Sir Rowell standing at the foot of the throne. She quickened her steps to get away from the mass of moving bodies. Yet, no matter how long or how fast she walked, she could not seem to reach her destination.

One by one, her friends looked at her with disappointment and left.

"Wait! Come back!" she yelled after them.

They paid her no heed.

All she could do was watch as they turned their backs to her and disappeared out of sight.

Abruptly, the music came to a stop.

Emilia looked around. No longer were the nobles dancing. They, too, flocked to the exit. "We better leave, she is cursed."

Their words reached her ears, making her heart ache.

"The Church warned us she would bring ruin to our kingdom."

"She is unworthy of the crown."

"No one wished for a useless child to lead us."

She covered her ears and screamed, "You're wrong! I'm innocent. I did nothing wrong!" Her eyes stung with tears as she sank to her knees. "Please come back, Ambrose, Lionhart, Sir Rowell…"

Despite her heartfelt pleas, the room emptied, and the lights flicked off. Dark shadows of the trees outside swayed with the wind and crept along the marble floor of the ballroom towards her.

Emilia pushed back the tears and scrambled away on all fours.

She wasn't fast enough.

The shadows caught up. They wrapped around her throat, wrists, and ankles, forming chains that kept her in place.

She yanked at the restraints around her neck. The more she tugged, the greater their hold became.

"You do not belong here," a childlike voice echoed in the room. "You will die here."

"You will die like us." This time, it was her eldest brother's voice.

"Why are you alive, Emilia?" the second brother bellowed. "Die. Die! Die! Like. Us."

Emilia broke out in a cold sweat. Ants crawled up her spine as she felt a hand gripping her shoulder. She turned her head to find the hostage boy from the funeral parade there.

The boy's cheeks were stained with bloody tears. He stared at her with the same horror as before. "You must die, Your Majesty. Die for us…"

She screamed.

Emilia shot upright in her bed, drenched in a cold sweat and clutching her dry throat. She had not had that nightmare in years. The orphan boy was an unwelcome addition.

"Bad dream?"

"Yes." Emilia frowned. The voice was too deep and husky to belong to Ambrose. Her head snapped in the direction of the man in question.

Moonlight streamed in from the balcony. The curtains had been pulled apart.

An unknown man clad in black leaned against the wall where the shadows were the thickest. His face was covered with a dark hood, making Emilia squint.

"An assassin?" She slowly reached under her pillow.

"Looking for this, Your Majesty?" A flash of silver in his hands was unmistakably her dagger.

"Why did you not kill me while I slept?"

"I would have if you were sleeping soundly. However, you seemed to be having quite a terrible time."

She arched a brow. "An assassin and a gentleman? Cute."

"This is the first time someone called me a gentleman." He took a silent step towards her bed. His fluid movements reminded her of a feline predator from one of the nature shows she used to watch in her previous life.

Emilia did not give up. She knew every item in her room, including anything that could be used as a weapon. Since her dagger was off-limits, she opted for the metal candlestick on the mantel as her next best option. While he was a few metres away, she lunged across her bed and ran to the mantel. Grabbing the candlestick, she barely managed to deflect his incoming attack.

The clanging of metal hitting metal rang in her ears.

As he pressed his dagger down, pushing the blade closer to her face, she asked, "Are you not afraid my guards will burst in at any moment?"

"I have drugged everyone on this floor, Your Majesty. No one will disrupt our dance."

And here I was hoping for some backup.

She ended up backed against the wall. Her shoulder burned, and she was positive that the searing pain from earlier was her wound reopening.

"Are you ready to die?" he asked in a light, mocking tone.

"How about I give you my first time and keep my life?"

"What?" He seemed taken aback. "I thought noblewomen were desperate to keep their chastity."

"In my world, nothing is too precious. This offer only extends if you have above-average looks."

"You are quite an interesting woman."

While he was failing to hold in his laughter, she pushed away from the wall and toppled him with all the force she could muster. In a mess of limbs, they fell on the floor with her straddling him and pressing the candlestick against his throat.

Between heavy pants, she asked, "Who sent you? Was it Malette? I swear I'll cut off his crown jewels when I see him again."

The assassin's hood fell back, revealing a handsome man in his mid-twenties. Her surprise lasted until he bucked and flipped them over, landing on top of her.

Using his weight to pin her down, he replied, "What was that? If my looks are above average, you would let me have your first time?"

A blush burned her cheeks. She defiantly glared at him, although most of him blended in with the shadows. "It is as I said. I would rather live and restore this kingdom than die with pointless dignity."

He inched back and studied her face. She could feel his hot breath on her skin. "You pass, Your Majesty."

"Pass what?"

He got up and offered her his hand. "This was a test to see if you would make a worthy master."

She swatted his hand away and groaned. The pain in her shoulder made her see spots.

"I do apologise for the damage you have sustained." He sounded apologetic. "Allow me to light a candle and attend to your wound."

"I don't understand." She pressed her hand against her bloodied shoulder and winced as sharp pain ricocheted across her spine. "Ow!"

"Pardon my rudeness." The assassin effortlessly lifted her into his arms and carried her to the bed. Having set her down, he lit multiple candles and brought them close enough to see the growing bloodstain on her nightgown.

Emilia kept her attention trained on his strange actions as if she was watching a movie and not participating in a ridiculous scenario.

"May I take a closer look?" he asked, his hand hovering next to her shoulder. There was no arousal or visible ill intent in his voice or expression.

Emilia sighed and peeled the material away from her wound, sliding it down her shoulder. "What did you mean by what you said?"

Their eyes met, and he pulled away after a quick assessment. For an assassin, he had pretty sky-blue eyes.

"I meant every word. I accept Your Majesty as the master of House Escariot." He went down on one knee next to her bed and lowered his head as his right fist touched his chest. "House Escariot pledges its blade and undying loyalty to Her Majesty, Queen Emilia Valeria Dante, from this day forth."

Her mouth fell open. Maybe she lost too much blood or was having a dream within a dream. Neither the pain in her shoulder nor the man in front of her melted away after her musing. So, she decided she was not losing her mind. Not yet, anyway.

"Wait, my father had assassins?"

"No. King Gilebert was deemed unworthy by the previous head of the house and so our representative never appeared before him."

"What made you think I was a worthy master?"

He cautiously raised his head but kept his eyes lowered. "We have witnessed how you protected the children at the parade. I apologise for testing your strength while you are injured. I wanted to wait until you recovered but too many people want you dead."

"And you are no longer one of them?"

"No, I am not."

"And your name?"

"I am Clayton Escariot X of the House Escariot. I have recently succeeded my late father, Clayton Escariot IX."

There was no record of a noble house with that name. Also, she could not recall a single mention of Escariot in any of Dante's history books.

Oh well, I've plenty of time to question him. She pointed to her shoulder. "Is there anything you can do about this before your master kicks the bucket?"

"Do I have your permission to work on your wound?"

She clenched her jaw as she recalled the awful pain from Lionhart's treatment. "Yes. Go ahead."

Clayton rummaged in a small satchel on his hip for a small vial of green liquid. "Drink this. It should numb the pain."

She popped the cap off and sniffed. It smelled putrid and not like anything that should be consumed by a human. "Are you sure this is not poison?"

"It can be used to stop someone's breathing if taken in a higher dose…"

Emilia swallowed nervously before downing the contents of the vial. "Urgh, this tastes as bad as it smells."

Clayton's lips quirked upwards. "Yes, it does."

Surprisingly, the effect of his medicine worked fast. The pain in her shoulder turned to numbness, and she grew sleepy.

He gently helped her lay her head on the pillow and sat on the bed next to her. "I forgot to mention, I am an ice and healing mage."

She yawned. "That's nice."

"Using my magic will be better than sealing the wound a second time." A golden flame began to dance on his palm. He pressed his hand against her shoulder, and the glow spread to her entire chest.

Through half-opened eyes, she watched him heal her wound. Whatever funky drugs he gave her did a wonderful job. She felt nothing from head to toe and could not care less if the ceiling collapsed or the room caught fire.

"Claaayton?" she drawled.

"Yes, Your Majesty?"

"When I see you again, you will be severely punished."

His cool fingers brushed her stray locks away from her forehead. "I will accept my punishment gladly."

"You are lucky you are handsome…" Finally, sleep welcomed her with open arms.

27
A NEW ADDITION

LAURENCE

When Laurence returned to the palace, something was off. The complete quiet was similar to visiting a cemetery at night.

He shuddered.

As he dragged his feet to his post, he found the Queen's guards lying on the ground, unconscious. He checked their pulse and breathing.

They're alive.

He gripped his sword's hilt and ran to the Queen's bedchambers. Prince Thessian would cut Laurence's wages if he failed his duty as the Queen's guard.

Bursting inside, he found Emilia lying on the bed and a strange man sitting next to her.

Laurence unsheathed his weapon and pointed it at the intruder. "What have you done to her?"

"Hmm? You must have been away from the palace, Sir Knight," the man replied nonchalantly. "As you can see, my master is safe and sound."

"What hogwash is that?" Laurence strode to the Queen's bedside and glanced at her sleeping face. Her clothes were slightly dishevelled but nothing was out of the ordinary. "Why isn't she waking up?"

"Because she is resting?" The stranger smacked Laurence's hand when he was about to check Emilia's pulse on her neck. He was on his feet in an instant with a dagger in hand. "Do not touch her with your filthy hands."

Laurence sensed this man would attack him if he got any closer.

What happened while I was away from the palace? More importantly, who is this questionable fellow?

"I need to make sure she is unharmed."

"She is. I healed her myself," the man replied.

"You are a mage?"

Since when did Emilia employ a mage? Laurence chuckled. There were plenty of secrets the Queen kept. The man before Laurence seemed like a loyal dog baring its teeth. He needed a tighter leash.

"What happened out there? Why are the guards asleep?" Laurence asked.

"Must I report everything to you? The only person who can order me around is Her Majesty. Now, leave and do not disturb her rest."

"As if I would let some strange man stay in her room all night." Laurence pointed towards the door. "If I am leaving, so are you."

The man sighed. "When she wakes, tell her I will be nearby." With that, he strode to the balcony and jumped over the balustrade.

Laurence rushed after him and peered over the edge to find no one below. "Another weird fellow appears…"

He eyed Emilia over his shoulder. Her chest rose and fell with steady intervals. He blew out a sigh of relief.

At least, she's alive.

He had to make a report to His Highness about the mage. No mere mage could jump off the second storey and disappear without a trace.

Behind him, he heard footsteps and turned around.

Ambrose paused with a bowl of water and some towels by the Queen's bed. "Oh, you are here too?"

Great. His well of information arrived. "Do you know who that man was?"

"You mean, Mister Clayton?"

Clayton? So that's his name. "Yes, him."

"He is Her Majesty's servant."

"Are you sure? I have never seen him around. Did he return from a mission?"

Ambrose set the tray on the end table by the bed and dabbed a white towel in the water. She placed the neatly folded towel on Emilia's forehead. "Her Majesty accepted his oath of loyalty. That is all that matters to me."

He scratched the back of his head. "You are telling me, a dangerous man appeared out of nowhere and swore an oath of loyalty to the Queen? What if his goal was to get close to her and kill her?"

"Then I would attempt to kill him."

"Attempt?"

"He is far more skilled in combat than I am," Ambrose admitted, caressing Emilia's cheek with her fingertips. "But I would gladly die for Her Majesty."

"And you left them alone to get water? What if he did something inappropriate to her?" Laurence's voice rose with disbelief. What was going on in Ambrose's head? Wasn't she Emilia's most loyal servant? How could she trust a stranger who popped up out of the blue?

Ambrose speared him with a look of annoyance. "The only foul-minded person here is you, Sir Laurence. It is you I would be afraid to leave Her Majesty with." She marched over to him. Jabbing her finger at his chest, she muttered, "I heard you were acting quite *intimate* with Her Majesty while she was sleeping in the carriage."

Laurence blushed and stepped back. "I-I only wanted to help her get some sleep."

"Uh-huh." Ambrose's distrust was obvious.

Stepping around her, he inched closer to the exit. "Look, I only came here to make sure she was safe."

"She is quite safe with me. You may leave."

Laurence trudged out of the room and closed the door behind him. He rested his back against the nearby wall, assuming his post. "That maid has to be insane."

28
TRUST ISSUES

EMILIA

Emilia **opened her eyes** to a familiar ceiling. She wasn't dead. That was a good start.

She sat up and stretched. The pain in her shoulder was gone. Peeling back her nightgown, she saw that her wound was healed without any scarring.

"Wow, Clayton did a good job." Her hand froze as she focused on her sleepwear. This was not the same nightgown she wore. Her face burned with her rising anger. "Did he change me while I slept?"

The door to her room opened, and Ambrose glided in. "You are finally awake, Your Majesty."

"Did you happen to see an assassin last night?"

Ambrose tilted her head to one side. "Are you referring to Mister Clayton?

"Yes. Where is he? If he changed my clothes while I slept, I will punch him in that handsome face of his."

"I did that."

"Oh..." Emilia climbed out of bed and hid her blushing cheeks behind the veil of her long hair. She cleared her throat. "Never mind then."

Ambrose's cheerfulness returned. "Would you like for your meal to be served here or in the dining hall?"

"The dining hall. I cannot stay cooped up in my room every morning." Since the fight with Clayton made her break a sweat, she pointed to the bathroom. "First, I need a bath."

"I will prepare it now." Ambrose skipped away to do her duties.

Curious, Emilia trailed behind her maid. "What put you in such a good mood?"

"I am happy because you are healed, Your Majesty. It pained me greatly to see you suffer."

"Thank you, Ambrose." As a test, Emilia spun her arms around.

Everything worked as it should. She grinned. *Magic is amazing.* She should have searched for a mage instead of avoiding them. Now, with Clayton on her side, she would get VIP healing treatment for free.

She looked around once more while Ambrose selected oil for the bath. "Where did he go?"

"Mister Clayton had a disagreement with Sir Laurence and left."

Emilia nearly rolled her eyes. Laurence could piss anyone off. She was amazed Clayton managed to keep his cool long enough to leave without altercation. "Sir Laurence is lucky to be alive."

"That he is."

Emilia rested her shoulder against the door frame. "What do you think of Clayton?"

"He is a skilled mage and fighter."

"That is not what I meant."

Ambrose smiled. "He treats you as he should while that dog—" Ambrose cut off what she wanted to say and smiled politely. "You will be safer with Mister Clayton by your side."

Emilia was dumbfounded. Ambrose never accepted the people

around Emilia with such ease. *Did Clayton give her a strange drug?* "Why do you trust him so much?"

"He healed you and kept away the pests in my absence. What is there not to like?"

"Pests?" Emilia made a mental note to query Sir Rowell about a possible rat problem in the palace. An infestation could be dangerous, especially at a time when medical treatment was centuries behind what she was used to and healing mages weren't scattered at every street corner.

After her morning routine, Emilia enjoyed a stroll through the gardens. The birds were chirping a cheerful tune, and the sun warmed her skin despite the chilly weather. She sucked in a lungful of winter air.

Ah, life sure is beautiful when nothing hurts!

"You seem happy," Laurence commented from a short distance away.

Here comes the burning meteor. "Good afternoon to you, too, Sir Laurence."

"I heard you were healed by a mage. Where did you find him?"

Emilia raised a brow. "What right do you have to question me?"

"He is too dangerous to keep around. What will you do if he betrays you?"

"Ambrose approves of him, so I need not worry."

He scoffed. "What would a mere maid know?"

Emilia stormed over and jabbed her finger into his chest. "You dare insult one of my people? Do I go around questioning why Prince Thessian is keeping a busybody like you?"

He pressed his lips together.

"I am heading to my office. Do not follow me." She walked off.

Her blissful morning was utterly ruined. She wasn't stupid. Of course, she knew loyalty did not come from nowhere. She was certain Clayton Escariot had a reason for becoming her servant. But Ambrose was no fool, either. She accepted him without a second thought, which meant he had no ill will towards Emilia. In the end, Emilia trusted her maid's judgement.

Well, a small test of loyalty should be fine, right?

Emilia arrived in her office to find a foreigner waiting for her. She stopped in the doorway, staring at the man's attire that came from Dante, but his skin was as dark as Lionhart's.

Could they be from the same continent?

"Are you going to stare at me all day?" He sounded like Lionhart as well. That couldn't be right. This man was clean-shaven and his hair was tied back with a ribbon like that of any noble.

The wheels in her head finally came to a halt, and she gasped, "Lionhart?"

"The one and only." He gave her a smile that could melt a maiden's heart.

"But you look so nice and proper... I even mistook you for a foreign envoy!"

"I shaved and brushed my hair, Emilia. There is no need for the theatrics."

Emilia raised her hands. "Wait here. I am going to get Ambrose. She must see this!"

"You can't be serious."

Emilia asked the guard at the door to fetch Ambrose. While she waited for her maid to arrive, she sat at her desk, unable to tear her eyes away from the changed man. "I knew you had that 'mysterious stranger' look going on, but I never thought you would be this attractive. Had I been younger, I would fall for you."

"You are almost eighteen. Are you implying I can only attract children?"

"Sorry, I meant older."

Emilia couldn't tell him that her mental age was that of a forty-year-old spinster. She had never had a boyfriend in either of her lives. Now, with handsome guys popping out of the woodwork, she could consider dating once she finished helping Thessian. Though, Lionhart was like an older brother and mentor to her.

Prince Thessian was her book crush but not someone she could date. When he becomes emperor, she would be stuck in the imperial palace as empress if they got married. That would destroy any hope for the freedom she craved. Laurence, although easy on the eyes, would drive her to spousal murder. And she knew next to nothing about Clayton.

Her shoulders slumped. *Am I destined to be alone forever? Where the hell is my Prince Charming with a six-pack? Like in those old romance novels, he would ride in on a white steed, wearing ornate silver armour, and fight off a hundred bandits to save me. Then, I would take his helmet off, and we would passionately—*

"You have that disturbing look on your face again," Lionhart commented as he plopped onto a sofa nearby.

"Yes, well, that is how my face is. Get used to seeing it often, Spymaster."

He cringed at his new title. "I promised to help you, and I will as long as I don't have to deal with the nobles directly."

"Fear not. Sir Rowell is fantastic at keeping them at bay. So far, aside from Count Baudelaire, I have not seen a single noble."

"Do you think the Duke's supporters are plotting something?"

Her smile faded. "I feel they will make their move soon. That is why I need your help. Gather as much information as you can on the corrupt officials and nobles in the kingdom. I want them to fall in one fell swoop."

"That is a tall order. You do not have a military big enough to execute such a show."

She drummed her fingers on the desk. "I may need to rely on Prince Thessian's and Count Baudelaire's men for this."

"Is it a good idea to entrust those men with so much power?"

She shrugged. "I am a monarch in name only. My goals are simple. Fix the kingdom, help Thessian win the Empire's crown, and retire to a piece of land of my own. Should I ask for a small county with a temperate climate?"

Lionhart frowned. "I didn't realise you were planning to leave your kingdom to the Hellion Empire."

"Trust me, it is for the best."

He did not reply.

The silence stretched until Ambrose came in. "Your Majesty, you wanted to see me?"

Emilia smiled brightly. "Yes. Look. Do you recognise this man?" She motioned to Lionhart.

Ambrose took one look at him. Without a change in her expression, she replied, "That is Mister Lionhart."

Emilia tried her best not to gape. "How could you recognise him with one glance?"

"His posture, figure, weight, and skin colour all indicate that it is him."

Lionhart laughed. "Your maid is better at reading people than you."

Emilia pouted. "Thank you, Ambrose. Sorry for disturbing you while you are in the middle of adapting to your new position."

"I am always happy to be called on by you, Your Majesty. Please never apologise for doing so."

"I will try to remember that." Once Ambrose left the office, Emilia asked Lionhart, "Have you heard anything about House Escariot?"

"They are a group of assassins that call themselves a family. Why? Did you come in contact with them?"

Clayton's family had to be quite famous for Lionhart to know of them off the top of his head. "Clayton Escariot pledged his loyalty to me last night."

Lionhart stared at her. Eventually, he blinked. "He did what?"

"Do you know of any connection between the Dante and Escariot families?"

"Shouldn't you be the one answering that question?"

She got up and walked to the window. "According to Clayton, a representative of the house comes to assess their future master only if they deem them worthy enough. He said I passed his test. So, I guess, I am his new master."

"House Escariot is known for completing any mission they accept. No matter who their target is or how well they hide, they will get to them. Be careful the dog you keep does not bite you."

Was Laurence's warning from earlier out of genuine concern instead of malice? He could have chosen better words, but still, she had to remain vigilant with a famous band of assassins by her side.

She rested her back against the windowsill. "Do they take on any contract that comes their way?"

"As far as I am aware, the target must have committed a grave sin or they will not touch them."

"So, they are what? Assassins with a Robin Hood complex?"

Lionhart's brows scrunched together. "What? Robin who?"

She wanted to smack herself on the forehead. Of course, Lionhart didn't know Robin Hood. They were both fictional characters.

Wait, I am a fictional character, too. Ugh, my head hurts from all this thinking. "I meant, are they the good kind of people?"

He gave her a sideways look. "As good as any killer out there, I suppose."

Emilia groaned and threw her hands up. "You are impossible. You know exactly what I am trying to say!"

"I do. And my answer remains the same. A killer is a killer, no matter their goals."

"Very well. I will be careful."

The soldier outside knocked and announced, "Lord Clayton Armel is seeking an audience with you, Your Majesty."

Was Armel the assassin's real name? She moved to her desk and sat down. "Let him in."

Clayton sauntered into the room with the same grace he showed during their fight. Instead of his assassin garb, he wore a bespoke embroidered charcoal coat with a pair of matching tanned leather boots. Last night, she did not get a chance to get a good look at him. While it was fashionable among the nobles to grow their hair out, he kept his raven hair past his square jawline. The eyes that seemed sky-blue in the candlelight were actually a startling light grey. The main attraction—his face—was a ten out of ten.

Emilia cleared her throat to regain her composure. "What brings you here, Lord Armel?"

He dropped onto one knee and lowered his head. "I came here

for my punishment, Your Majesty."

Emilia vaguely remembered mentioning a severe punishment last night. After he healed her, she was nothing but grateful, even if her old wound reopened at one point during their fight.

"Lord Armel, please rise. I would like to introduce you to a friend of mine." She made her way to where Lionhart was sitting. "This is Lionhart. He will be taking on the position of Spymaster starting today."

Clayton offered his hand to Lionhart in a form of a handshake. "Mister Lionhart, it is always a pleasure to meet another man of the same craft."

Emilia did a double-take. "What? You were an assassin?"

Lionhart shook hands with Clayton, but the atmosphere changed from pleasant to frosty in an instant. "You did not need to reveal that, boy."

"As my master's friend, you should not keep such a dangerous secret to yourself. What if she trusted you too much and you stabbed her in the back?"

Emilia saw their hands shaking from how hard they gripped one another. She thought she would hear bones breaking any minute, so she pushed them apart.

"I trust you both to be civil." Facing Lionhart, she said, "I suspected you had a past. I do not mind if you were an assassin or a mercenary." She directed her next words at Clayton. "Lord Armel, you should be careful. Upsetting my friends is a good way to get on my bad side."

He lowered his head. "I do apologise for my rudeness, Mister Lionhart, Your Majesty."

Emilia clasped her hands together and beamed at them. "Shall we have some tea?"

Pleased her guests settled their disagreement, she called for Sir Rowell, who promptly had everything organised to perfection.

Before she knew it, Emilia was enjoying rose tea from the Hellion Empire and talking about the ton of paperwork she needed to get through. Each breath she took was a joy to her senses. Sadly, her serenity had to end. A test of loyalty had to be conducted sooner rather than later.

The Queen placed her teacup on the saucer and pushed them away. "Lord Armel, I want to know how loyal House Escariot is to me."

Clayton followed her lead and set his cup aside. He placed his hands on his knees and lowered his head. "Master, may I ask we speak about this in private?"

Emilia bit her lip. The test she wanted to conduct could endanger her. Having Lionhart there would be of great benefit. The downside was that she would need to expose the contents of the deal between the Dante and Escariot families to an outsider. She weighed the pros and cons.

"Lionhart will remain. Please understand my caution."

Lionhart spoke up. "Don't worry. I can keep a secret or two."

Clayton seemed disappointed. "I will follow your wishes, Master. To answer your question, the ancient contract dictates that a master can request anything, including this servant's life and it must be given."

What kind of insane contract did his ancestor sign? "If I asked you to kill yourself here and now, you would do it, no questions asked?"

"Yes."

The next part was going to be the hardest. Emilia put on her best poker face and said, "Do it then."

For a fraction of a second, Clayton's fingers dug into his knees. His body tensed. "Please give me a weapon."

"You are an ice mage, are you not?" Emilia tried to sound ruthless. "Make a weapon with your magic."

He lifted his right hand. Steam began to rise from his palm as shimmering ice particles formed above it. She stared in wonder at the process. Mages were fascinating. In a way, she wanted a few more on her side if she could see more tricks like that.

It took less than ten seconds for him to create a replica of the dagger she kept under her pillow.

Clayton pointed the dagger at his heart and waited. "Please give me your final command."

Judging by the resigned expression on his face, and the strong grip with which he held the ice dagger, she knew he would execute her command flawlessly and ruin her furniture and carpet with his blood.

Emilia placed her hand over his and pushed his arm down. "I rescind my command. Be at ease, Lord Armel."

He dropped the dagger onto the seat next to him and let out a heavy breath. "Seems Master has a terrible sense of humour."

Emilia lifted her hand. "It is getting tiresome with you calling me that all the time. Use my title instead."

"I will oblige, Your Majesty," Clayton said with a charming smile.

Too bad her current world did not have mobile phones. She would have snapped a picture of his face and used it as her wallpaper. He was too cute when the dimples in his cheeks appeared.

Focus, Emilia. He is just one man. "Your real task is to find a man who used to go by the name of Julio Grande and bring him to me."

Lionhart scowled. "Our guild is in the process of locating him."

"Have you ever heard of the expression 'first come first served'?"

"No," Lionhart said.

Emilia grinned. "It means, whoever finds him first wins." She looked at Clayton. "Can you do it?"

"Should he be captured alive or will his body suffice?" Clayton asked matter-of-factly.

"Alive."

"I will find him for you before the Lionhart Guild does."

"Don't get cocky, boy." Lionhart smirked. "We have over two hundred members. You, on the other hand, possess a handful of assassins."

Clayton let out a soft chuckle that unnerved Emilia. "We can find any prey, Mister Lionhart, be they dead, undead, or alive."

Lionhart leaned forward in his seat. "Bold words for a mere child."

"I have not been a child from the moment I killed my first mark at the age of nine."

"Ha! I killed my first at seven," Lionhart retorted.

"Being out of the death business for so long has aged you. Leave these matters to the experts."

"Experts, you say?" Lionhart let out a loud guffaw. "Where? I don't see any here."

"Err... Gentlemen?" Her voice was drowned out by their ongoing tirade. "Hello?" She picked up her teacup and finished her drink. Their argument kept heating up, so she clapped her hands. "Gentlemen!"

The room fell silent as the duo stared at her apologetically. They were like two big dogs that got scolded by their owner. She could almost see the tucked tails and droopy ears.

"I am glad that is over." She smiled politely. "I suggest you two stop bickering and get to work. Lionhart, you have yet to go over the records of your predecessor and establish your network within these walls and beyond. Find all of the nobles who are siding with Duke Malette and begin gathering evidence against them. Lord Armel, find Julio and bring him here alive. You may leave."

"Yes, Your Majesty," they replied in unison.

"See?" she said cheerfully. "You two can get along."

29
WAVERING SUPPORT

THESSIAN

It was dawn when Thessian arrived at camp. With heavy eyelids, he was ready for a good rest.

He dragged his feet to his tent and was about to collapse on his bed when a noise alerted him that someone had entered his tent.

"Your Highness," Sir Ian began in an apologetic tone, "an important missive has arrived."

Thessian groaned as he sat on the edge of his bed and looked at his knight.

Unlike most of the people in Thessian's elite unit, Sir Ian was not from Hellion. He hailed from Shaeban, an ally kingdom north of the Hellion Empire. His hair, eyes, and skin were so pale that Ian often hid them along with his pointed ears. Today, Thessian was hit with the full view of the Pale Man without his headscarf.

"Can this not wait until after I get some well-deserved rest?"

"It's from your supporters in Dante."

Thessian beckoned for Sir Ian to hand over the letter. After breaking the seal, he skimmed the contents. The nobles wished for an urgent meeting.

Are they looking down on me?

Thessian raked his fingers through his locks. He needed their support to retain a strong military presence in Dante and secure the supply chains. "Tell Ronne to keep watch on the duke's men and report any changes in their behaviour to Laurence. You and I will be leaving for Redford shortly."

"Redford? Isn't that Count Fournier's territory?"

"It is. Prepare supplies for a day's journey and ready the horses. We leave in two hours."

Ian lowered his head and stepped out of Thessian's tent.

Had Sir Ian Black been better at voicing his opinions, he may have been Thessian's second-in-command instead of Laurence. At present, no one other than Laurence had the stones big enough to scold Thessian or the skill to keep the chatty Hellion nobles at bay. Laurence's unquestionable ability with the sword was not something to dismiss, either. They did manage to defeat those twenty bandits four years ago. However, somehow, the rumour turned it into one hundred. Or was it two hundred?

Thessian never did find out how that happened.

After a brief nap and a quick meal, Thessian was ready to go.

With the addition of his advance forces, the number of men in his camp exceeded two hundred. Additional rows of black tents were set up to keep his soldiers from the cold.

Most of them were outside, cleaning their weapons, eating, or engaged in conversation. They grew silent and saluted when Thessian walked past them.

Thessian acknowledged his men with a nod. The bustling

activity reminded him of his years on the battlefield. The only difference was that there was no enemy to fight yet. The coup was more successful than he had originally anticipated. Emilia made a good partner and a useful regent. Without Marquess Walden's military support present, a full-on fight against Duke Malette's forces could cause Thessian quite a headache. He trusted Emilia would use her connections if push came to shove. Together, they had a better chance of stomping down any rebellion before it gained traction and turned into a true civil war.

"The preparations are complete, Your Highness," Sir Ian informed him. He was back to wearing a headscarf that covered most of his face.

"Good. Let's head out."

They mounted their horses and rode away from the camp. A bristling, cold wind whipped around Thessian as they followed the snow-covered roads. The fur he wore did almost nothing to keep out the chill that penetrated down to his skin and bone. He gripped the leather reins harder. Dante's winters were colder than in the Empire where it hardly ever snowed. When all was said and done, he would dig out a bottle from his reserve and have a drink in a nice hot bath.

I did promise to share it with Emilia...

Thessian nearly diverted his horse as his thoughts headed in a dangerous direction. He was becoming like Laurence, with a mind filled with useless ideas. But he was no monk. He, too, needed to relieve his sexual frustration now and then. After things had settled down, he could visit the Golden Suns with Laurence. A trip to the Empire's most famous brothel should be payment enough for his friend's hard work on this mission.

After riding until the horses could not take it anymore, Thessian and Sir Ian stopped in a small village and spent the night at a tavern for some rest.

The next day, they kept pushing the horses until they could see the high stone walls of Redford bathed in the rays of the setting sun. From what Thessian heard on the road, Redford was often plagued by monsters that descended the Hollow Mountains. They were few, but, every so often, a pack of ice wolves would appear and attack the farmers. That was why Count Fournier had plenty of archers stationed on the battlements.

A soldier in full armour at the gate raised his hand. "Halt! We need to see some identification."

Thessian pulled out the letter with the Count's seal and showed it to the guard. "I am here by invitation from Count Fournier. He is expecting me."

The guard carefully studied the seal and handed the letter back. "We were informed of some important guests arriving. Please head to the castle."

Thessian nudged his horse forward.

They entered through the gates to find a town bustling with life. Compared to the gloom hanging over Newburn, Redford was full of smiles and laughter. Children played games and chased one another.

For a town often invaded by monsters, they seemed happy. Upon closer inspection, Thessian could tell that most men were quite muscular under their winter clothes. The women, too, seemed like they could beat a bandit in a fistfight.

Halfway up the road to the castle, they were met with a guard captain and his men.

The captain removed his helmet and lowered his bald head in greeting. "Your Grace, I am Captain Neil Gagnon. Thank you for coming on such short notice to our humble territory. We apologise for not having the time to organise a proper welcome."

"I did not come here for entertainment." Having a mere count summon Thessian as if he was his lapdog was insulting enough. Dante's nobility needed to be taught a lesson but not today. He had to maintain a good relationship with them. As long as they allowed his army to march through their lands, he could keep his hold over the kingdom. "Where is Lord Fournier?"

"He's in the dining hall. You may leave your horses here and follow me."

Thessian nodded to Ian, who climbed off his horse and handed the reins to the nearest soldier. Thessian patted his dark horse on the neck and did the same.

During the stroll through the castle, he picked up on several things. One—Count Fournier had a large family and liked to commission paintings every time there was an addition. Two—the lord was not big on displaying his wealth, unlike the other nobles. And finally, there was an overwhelming number of stuffed animals and monster heads mounted on the walls. Quite a number of furnishings, as well as the chandeliers, were fashioned out of tusks, horns, and antlers.

Captain Gagnon pushed open the double doors that led to a large dining hall. A strong smell of roast meat and potatoes hung thick in the air. Dozens of candles lit the hall, painting the dull, grey walls a golden shade. Unlike the rest of the castle, the hall was decorated with weapons and axes from all over the continent, some of which the prince did not recognise.

Thessian spotted familiar faces from his initial dealings with the Dante nobility. They were all lords who supported the coup.

Count Edgar Fournier was a burly, bearded man who topped Thessian in height by three inches. He stood out among the rest of the nobles like a mountain in the middle of small hills. Over his navy tunic, he wore the fur of an ice wolf that shimmered like ice crystals in the light.

Seeing Thessian, Lord Fournier squeezed past the nobles and smiled. "Duke of Darkgate, welcome to my humble abode!"

Had Thessian not been summoned in such a rude manner, he may have returned the smile. Instead, he kept his expression straight. "Lord Fournier, I assumed you had urgent business with me as your letter implied."

"Straight to business? You remind me of my younger self." Lord Fournier graciously motioned for Thessian to follow. "Please, take a seat at the table. As host, I must feed my guests before any business takes place, as per tradition here."

Thessian reluctantly complied. As he took his seat at the long oak table, Ian moved to stand guard with his hands folded behind his back.

"Pour His Grace some ale!" Lord Fournier ordered his servants cheerfully.

Sitting next to Thessian was Marquess Carrell who controlled Dante's northern border and was in charge of the Northern Watchtower. Although the Marquess was a seasoned warrior in his younger years, King Gilebert kept him out of any military decisions since taking the throne. He was also the first man to back Thessian's invasion plan. "Have you been well, Your Grace?"

"Quite well. Thank you, Lord Carrell," Thessian replied as a manservant poured ale into his silver goblet.

"As you may have guessed, we may not get down to business tonight. Lord Fournier enjoys his drink too much during gatherings."

Thessian stared at the amber liquid in his goblet. He could insist they move on to an important matter yet chose against it. He was in no hurry. The Lionhart Guild was searching for Julio Grande, Emilia was informed of Duke Malette's recent movements, and Ronne was keeping watch on the Duke's small force outside of Newburn.

Finally able to relax, Thessian raised his goblet. "A few drinks never hurt anyone."

"That's right!" Lord Fournier shouted from his seat at the heart of the table. "Let us drink the night away!"

The loud cheers of the lords drowned out the dissatisfied grunts of the minority. Eventually, even the ones who seemed reluctant were too drunk to care.

Lord Fournier's wife, Countess Estelle Fournier, who seemed much more delicate than the rest of the women in town, appeared used to her husband's lively behaviour. She kept busy by chatting with the nearby guests.

Thessian spotted a handful of times where she pretended to drink, yet her throat did not move. Most likely, her alcohol tolerance was not as good as that of her husband. Thessian could not blame her. The ale he drank at Fournier's castle was one of the most potent drinks he had ever consumed. After three goblets, he felt the brew's strong pull and instinctively slowed his pace.

By midnight, half of the lords were unconscious on the table, and

Lord Fournier was urged by his wife to stop and head to bed. Luckily for everyone involved, Lord Fournier listened to his well-meaning wife.

Thessian rubbed his aching eyes.

Sir Ian arrived at his side. "I was told you could use one of the rooms to get some rest. Would you like me to escort you?"

"Please do."

Marquess Carrell caught Thessian by the upper arm. He quickly realised what he had done and jerked his hand away. "Apologies, Your Grace. I was too eager in wanting to speak with you before you retire."

"Come to the courtyard, Lord Carrell. It seems we both need fresh air."

The Marquess slipped out of his seat with no trouble, which told Thessian that he was pretending to be drunk throughout the evening.

In the courtyard, where the stars shone bright and the large moon even brighter, the snow-covered trees swayed in the gentle breeze.

Marquess Carrell took a seat on a stone bench and said, "My old friend sure knows how to force his guests into a drunken stupor."

"It is uncommon for nobles to get drunk in Hellion during formal events," Thessian admitted, joining him on the bench. "I, for one, prefer this welcome to a formal one."

"I think Edgar would be happy to hear that." Lord Carrell looked at Thessian with interest. "I must ask, Your Grace, how did the coup go? When we heard the princess survived and took over, we were beginning to fear the worst."

"There has been a slight change in management but that is all."

Carrell's bushy brows scrunched together. "Is the young princess your new regent? Why? She has no experience or formal education in ruling a nation. Hasn't she spent her entire life in a tower?"

Thessian chuckled. He had thought the same about Emilia at first. *How wrong was I?* "I am certain she will surprise you."

"Do you trust her?"

Thessian did not give his trust away for nothing. The time he spent with Emilia was short yet enjoyable. She was an interesting companion and full of surprises. "I do. Enough to leave this kingdom in her capable hands for the time being. She is approachable and easy to get along with. If you do not believe me, feel free to arrange a meeting."

"I believe in your judgement," Lord Carrell said with a nod. "You have won many great battles in recent years and appear to be a good judge of character. I will continue to support you."

"You have my thanks."

The Marquess coughed into his gloved hand. "I heard rumours that her appearance is quite lacking. Is that true?"

Thessian burst into laughter. The alcohol had loosened him up. He wiped at the stray tear in the corner of his eye. "It is quite the opposite. She is beautiful enough to have my second-in-command go on about her appearance for days."

"I guess, you cannot believe everything you hear. And here I thought you had your ally, Marquess Walden, killed on his arrival in Dante."

The drunken haze Thessian enjoyed was gone in an instant. "Where did you hear that from?"

"Two maids, claiming to be servants of Lady Diane Walden, were captured in a nearby village. They declared that Your Grace drugged and killed Walden's soldiers."

Thessian balled his hands in his lap. "Where are they now?"

"Their story was so unbelievable that Edgar had them put in jail." Lord Carrell's piercing stare felt like knives were being stabbed into the side of Thessian's head. "From your reaction, I can see that particular rumour had a bit of truth to it."

"I had no choice." Thessian combed his hand through his hair. "Walden betrayed me. There was plenty of evidence of bribery." There was no reason to reveal that the person who did the bribing was Thessian's younger brother.

Lord Carrell got up and shoved his hands into the pockets of his trousers. "I do not blame you, Your Grace. I would have done the same."

"Do you think this will affect my support base?"

"To be quite frank, Baron Niel and Marquess Thibault may openly frown upon this, but they would be too afraid to back out. Marquess Chupert, Marquess Rigal, Edgar and I think very much alike. We will not fault you for eliminating a problem before it arises. In fact, we welcome such steadfast action from our future king."

Thessian rose to his full height, looming over Lord Carrell. "From the start, while Lord Fournier played the role of a drunken host, your job was to get the answers to what the others wanted to know."

"You are, indeed, quite a perceptive man," Lord Carrell complimented with a sly smile. "Worry not. Those maids will be silenced and the rumours squashed."

"This makes my job here easier. You have yourself a good night, Lord Carrell."

"I thank you for your consideration, Your Grace."

30
NIGHT VISITORS

EMILIA

Emilia **retired to her bedchambers** for the night. She sat on the bed, mulling over the report Sir Laurence gave her about Duke Malette's additional men assembling within the city walls. There was a good chance he would try to sneak in the rest of his soldiers from the outside and attempt a coup of his own. She couldn't let that happen. Her head on a spike on the castle walls was not a picture she enjoyed painting in her mind's eye.

Why can't I have a day where nothing happens? Is that too much to ask?

A knock on her balcony door startled her out of her reverie.

She recognised the silhouette immediately. "You may enter, Clayton."

The new addition to her team slipped into her room. This time, he wore normal clothes, unlike on the night of her test. "Your

Majesty, I came to report on the progress of my mission."

"Surely, you could not have found Julio already?"

He smirked. "I have. He is being detained by my sister and her men in a house near Main Street."

"How did you manage to track him down by his name alone?" She could not hide how impressed she was by the efficiency of House Escariot. In a way, she was glad she was not their mark.

"We keep tabs on every person closely related to the royal family. From the day of his arrival at the palace until this day, that man was being observed in secret."

"Why did you not tell me this earlier?"

"We had to verify his identity, Your Majesty."

She crossed her arms. They probably tortured the information out of Julio. A tiny part of her felt pity for the man. With this done, all she had to do was hand him over to Thessian. Hopefully, he will be pleased enough to stop looking like he was ready to lynch everyone in his vicinity.

"There is one more thing I was meaning to ask you. Why is House Escariot in servitude to Dante's Royalty? Why not take off and void the ancient contract?"

Clayton seemed hesitant to reply. He walked to a painting of the previous queen, who died after giving birth to Emilia, and looked at it in silence.

When he was done gathering his thoughts, he faced her. "The story is not grand or interesting, Your Majesty. My ancestor, Clayton Escariot I, committed a grave sin against the founding king. So, the king employed a powerful mage to put a curse on our family. For ten generations, we must serve a master of Dante's blood and obey every command. We were given a single sliver of freedom. The master can only be chosen by the head of the house. If a master is not selected in that generation, the head of the house will end their duty, often there and then."

"Without a master, you have to kill yourself?" she asked, incredulous.

"Yes and no. Should we forego killing ourselves, the curse will see to it that we perish."

She stared at him in disbelief. Emilia's ancestor was a real nut, even if he was the founder of the kingdom. "You are the last head bound by the deal, correct?"

"Yes, Your Majesty."

How unlucky! And here I thought I was the only one with a dreadful backstory. "Can a master release you from your duty of their own free will?"

He seemed confused by her question. "No one ever considered letting us go. I do not know what will happen if you abandon me."

"Looks like we will need to dig up that ancient contract and have a look at it."

"There is no need to look for it." Clayton started unbuttoning his coat and then his shirt.

"Wait! Why are you stripping?" She covered her eyes but could not resist peeking through the gaps between her fingers.

Ah, men with abs are the best!

He dropped the clothes on the floor and turned around.

Long lines of ink were tattooed into his broad back. The contract was written in an ancient runic language she could not read or understand.

She ran her fingers over the bold symbols, grazing his warm skin that had a multitude of scars under the elaborate tattoo. "Do you know how to read this?"

"Over the centuries, this particular language of the mages was lost. From my grandfather's generation, we are all relying on a translation provided by the Mage Assembly."

The Mage Assembly was a topic Emilia knew next to nothing about. Outwardly, King Gilebert seemed disinterested in magic to the point where he had his servants burn historical books about mages as well as anything else relating to magic. But then, why did he house a magic researcher from Hellion in his home for so many years? Something didn't feel right about the entire situation.

Emilia picked up his shirt and handed it to him. She stole one last peek at his defined muscles and broad shoulders. "Get dressed. You must be getting cold."

"Thank you." Much to her disappointment, he was dressed in

less than a minute.

"Is there a chance the mages mistranslated or omitted information?"

"We would not know," he admitted. "We can only rely on what we were given."

"Hmm… As there is nothing we can do about your curse at present, we should focus on other things."

As she was heading back to her bed, Clayton caught her wrist, drawing her attention. "Why would Your Majesty want to break my family's curse? A servant who cannot disobey is ideal."

She shook off his loose grip. "I do not think highly of slavery or indentured servitude. I would rather you served me out of your own free will."

"I chose you to be my master on my own."

"Would you have come here to seek me out if you were not cursed?"

He lowered his gaze. "I suppose not."

"Once we figure out how to break that pesky curse, you can do whatever you want. Until then—" she placed a hand on his shoulder and smiled, "—I will be in your care."

The tips of his ears turned red. He kept his face lowered as he stepped out of her reach. "Is there anything else Your Majesty wishes for me to do?"

"I would like for you to retrieve a certain jailbreaker for me as quietly as possible."

He lifted his head but did not meet her eyes. "Are you referring to Duke Malette?"

"Yes. Initially, I wanted to wait until his supporters showed themselves. It looks like waiting any longer would be a mistake. He has been a busy boy, gathering forces under my nose while assembling an army in his territory."

"Should the situation not work out in my favour, am I permitted to eliminate his guards?"

"There is no point in needlessly endangering yourself. I would prefer to reduce the casualties, but it cannot be helped if they attack first."

"I will leave at once."

"Wait!" Emilia called out when he was about to set foot on the balcony. "Find Jehan and Ernesto. They are members of the Lionhart Guild who are watching the duke's hideout. They should have noticed the patterns in his security. Tell them Lady Em sent you."

"Lady Em?"

"It is my alias for dealings outside of the palace."

He nodded and jumped over the edge of her balcony.

Emilia fell backwards onto her lavender-scented sheets, spreading her arms out. The men in her life were a strange bunch. One burst into her room whenever he pleased and the other climbed to her balcony just to give her a report.

"Should I put up a 'NO MEN AFTER MIDNIGHT' sign?" As tempting as her idea was, she doubted Thessian would bother to pause long enough to read it. On the other hand, Clayton might miss it entirely in the darkness. "I could get a guard dog instead."

31

THE LOWER, THE BETTER

LAURENCE

Laurence lay on a round bed, surrounded by red silk sheets. Female laughter in the room brought a smile to his face as he stroked the smooth, rose-coloured hair of an elven maiden.

She lifted her head from the bed, and her plump lips inched into a naughty smile.

Another girl's blonde head peered through the dividing curtain. She winked at him. "Would you like a sensual massage, Sir Knight?"

Laurence eagerly patted the space next to him. "Yes! Yes, I would. The lower, the better." He scooted over, allowing her to have access to his naked back.

The girl's soft hands caressed his lower back with masterful movements that removed all tension in his body.

He groaned with pleasure. "This is what life is about! No battles, no cruel orders for yours truly, and no—"

A beautiful belly dancer glided into the room of the Golden Suns. Her revealing clothes kept his attention on all the curves and valleys on her hourglass figure. As she danced, the golden silk tied around her wrists moved with her, making it seem like she had fairy wings.

He inched closer to the edge of the bed, forgetting the other beauties around him. The masked stranger had his full attention.

The dancer occasionally lifted her mysterious gaze at him.

Laurence sat rod-straight. He could not wait for the dance to end, so he could welcome her into his arms. If he had to pay extra, he would do it, no questions asked.

Finally, the girl came to a stop in a kneeling position on the ground. She sat on her haunches. Her rapid breathing had a mesmerising effect as her ample chest rose and fell to a tune of its own.

He invited her with open arms. "Come to me, my fairy."

The dancer gracefully climbed to her feet and swayed her hips on her way to him. She placed her hands on his shoulders, making the bangles on her wrists jingle. "I am too much for you to handle, dear customer..."

"Nonsense!" Laurence smirked and bumped his chest with his fist. "I can handle anything."

"Oh my..." She lifted her hands to the veil that covered most of her face and slowly peeled it away.

To match those alluring eyes, Laurence could make out the curve of her plump cherry lips. Then, his excitement began to simmer down as more of the dancer's face was revealed.

He shuddered and scrambled back to the other end of the bed. "What are YOU doing here?"

Ernesto winked. "You said you could handle me."

"No!" Laurence squealed. He coughed to clear his throat.

"There is no need to be shy." Ernesto climbed onto the bed. Instead of a woman's body, his shape became that of a slender man. He crawled along the bed towards Laurence.

The seductive act was lost on Laurence. He searched for the exit.

The other women and doors had vanished.

With unnatural strength, Ernesto pinned Laurence down, climbing on top of him with ease. "Shall we have some fun now, dear customer?"

Laurence's eyes shot open. He looked around, finding that he was in front of the Queen's bedchambers. In his exhaustion, he had fallen asleep on the job.

Holding his forehead with his hands, he mumbled, "What a nightmare!"

Out of nowhere, he heard a voice reply, "You make a terrible guard."

Whipping out his sword, he pointed it in the direction of the intruder. "Who is it?"

The Queen's trusted maid came over with a look of disgust on her youthful face. "I cannot believe a filthy-minded beast like you is guarding Her Majesty."

Did I talk in my sleep? "My mind is not filthy, and I cannot help being tired after running around for days with no rest."

Ambrose scoffed and proceeded to place her hand on the door handle to the Queen's room. She gave him one last withering look and disappeared inside.

Laurence bumped his head against the wall multiple times in the hopes he was still dreaming. Sadly, the current nightmare was as real as Ernesto's cross-dressing.

32
ATTACK OF THE BEASTS

THESSIAN

As expected, the mood of the lords after an evening of drinking was low. Much to Thessian's amazement, Lord Fournier was fresher than a daisy. During their breakfast, Lord Fournier talked with such gusto, that Thessian wondered if he had a magical cure for crapulence stashed away.

That morning, Fournier had also invited his five daughters to dine with them. They were fully dressed up and seated across from Thessian, which gave him a bad feeling. He was used to lords in the Hellion Empire attempting to lock him into matrimony with their offspring. The thought of having to leave a wife behind while he waged wars did not sit well with him. He had dismissed more than three dozen dainty ladies who had no concept of the world beyond the ballroom walls or high society. Talk of his time on the battlefield made them quickly lose interest.

"Your Grace, are you not enjoying your meal?" Lady Estelle Fournier asked from the seat next to her husband. She had encased her neck and ears in rubies and even put on lavish makeup.

"Not at all. This is one of the best hot meals I have had in weeks. It is delicious, Lady Estelle."

Thessian internally chided himself for allowing his emotions to show. He had been away from the Empire's court for too long. There, showing emotion was the same as displaying his weakness. Plenty of wolves in high society wanted to drag him off his hero pedestal. Somehow, with Laurence's help, Thessian managed to make his escape at the right time.

Am I missing my pesky subordinate?

Thessian briefly glanced at Sir Ian who stood guard two paces behind him. Sir Ian never complained. He hardly spoke unless it had to do with passing information along. Having him as a companion was proving to be rather dull.

"Do not be shy, Your Grace," Lord Fournier said with a toothy smile. "Eat your fill and tell your noble friends of the Redford hospitality!"

"I will."

Lord Carrell drank his ale quietly next to Thessian. They had exchanged a handful of words before the meal.

After filling his stomach, the tiredness from Lord Carrell's raddled face melted away. "I have spoken with the other lords. They are fine with Princess Emilia taking over as your regent as long as you oversee her decisions."

"When did you find the time to speak with them?"

"My night was quite busy, Your Grace." He leaned closer to Thessian's ear and whispered, "Be prepared. The moment this meal ends, run or make an excuse to escape."

Thessian played along and pretended he had not heard anything alarming. He faked a chuckle. "Lord Carrell, it is good to know you care so much for my well-being."

Lord Fournier raised his goblet in the air. "To family and friends!"

The rest of the lords grunted their agreement.

After the toast, Thessian was about to follow Marquess Carrell's advice when Lord Fournier rushed over with his daughters in tow.

"Too late..." Lord Carrell muttered under his breath.

Not this again. Thessian looked directly at the incoming group. "Lord Fournier, I was about to start preparations for my return. Should you have any questions about the events at the Dante palace ask Lord Carrell."

"I heard enough from him at dawn." Lord Fournier made a sweeping motion, showing off a line of girls who looked ready to fight a bear rather than meet a possible spouse. "I would like to introduce my daughters, Your Grace. From the left, this is Helga, Elga, Volga, Taiga, and Riga. Their ages are eighteen, seventeen, fifteen, thirteen, and twelve, I think..."

Volga clapped. "You did well, Papa."

Fournier's face reddened at the praise. "Thank you, dearest."

Thessian had a hunch that Lord Fournier was the one to name his daughters. One look at the embarrassed face of Lady Estelle confirmed his suspicion. "Good morning, ladies. I hope you have enjoyed your meal as much as I have."

The girls bowed their heads in greeting. Helga was the only one to comment on the meal while the others stole glances at Sir Ian.

"My daughters are not usually this shy." Lord Fournier fired them a disapproving look. "Girls, tell His Grace about your hobbies."

Thessian raised his hands. "Perhaps another time would be best suited..."

"No need to worry," Lord Fournier countered. "You will be impressed. I am certain of it! Go on, girls."

Helga went first. Her physique was on the sturdy side which matched her square face. "Your Grace, I am Lady Helga Fournier. I can gut and skin a bear in under thirty minutes."

Thessian's jaw nearly hit the floor. That was an impressive feat and introduction.

Lord Fournier let out a booming laugh. "See? I told you it would be good!"

Next, the slender daughter named Elga stepped forward. "I am

Lady Elga Fournier. I can hit an apple from fifty paces with my arrow."

Volga gave a brief curtsy and placed her hand on her chest. Fire lit in her green eyes as she announced, "Please pick me, Your Grace! No one in Redford can beat my speed. I can run faster than a calygreyhound!"

Thessian raised a brow. "Have you raced one, Lady Volga?"

She pouted. "Well, not a calygreyhound, no. I did outrun a group of goblins and an ice wolf before."

"That is impressive."

Volga beamed at Thessian. "Thank you, Your Grace!"

"My turn." Taiga nudged Volga aside. She was the only one who had feminine air to her. "I am Lady Taiga Fournier. My skills include embroidery, painting, and fencing."

Lady Estelle clapped from her seat and winked at her daughter.

Lord Fournier, on the other hand, urged his youngest to step forward.

Riga was up to Thessian's stomach in height. Long blonde waves framed her round face. Her clear hazel eyes reflected much uncertainty, and Thessian could not figure out why Lord Fournier brought her along. "Your Grace, I am Riga Fournier, and…and I like playing with fire."

"Papa, Riga is too young to be here," Volga complained.

"What do you mean? You are an adult when you kill your first bear in this house," Lord Fournier replied.

Thessian stared at the child in disbelief. How could such a small, fragile creature kill a bear before adulthood? "Surely, you jest."

"No." Lord Fournier hugged Riga against him. He ruffled her hair as he added, "Riga killed her first bear last month. I am so proud that I have commissioned a new painting just of her."

"You are spoiling her, Papa," Volga grumbled.

Riga retreated into the line-up and lowered her gaze. Her cheeks were flushed with a tinge of red.

Thessian backed up a step. "They are all lovely ladies but there are a lot of matters I must attend to in Newburn."

Lord Carrell joined the conversation. "Edgar, do not push your desires onto others. These girls will be a burden to His Grace on the battlefield. They are not trained knights."

"Battlefield?" Thessian frowned. "What are you talking about?"

"It is simple." Lord Carrell nodded toward his old friend. "Edgar desperately wishes for you to select one or two of his daughters and train them as your knights."

Relieved, Thessian chuckled. "So, this is not about marriage?"

"Marriage?" Lord Fournier scrunched up his brows. "How could you think that, Your Grace? My daughters are free to marry whomever they choose provided they kill a bear or capture a fire bird. It is the Fournier rite of passage that proves to others one is a true adult."

"Any thoughts, Your Grace?" Lord Carrell inquired with amusement lacing his voice.

Lord Fournier slapped his hands together and lowered his head. "Please, just take one!"

Thessian could not dismiss an ally's heartfelt request. He indicated over his shoulder at Sir Ian. "If any one of them can land a hit on my subordinate, I will consider taking them along."

Lord Fournier's and the girls' eyes gleamed. They bundled together into a circle, muttered a few things, and dispersed. The ladies walked away as fast as their dresses and rules of politeness permitted.

"They left to get changed," Lord Fournier clarified. He hollered to the rest of the lords and his men. "The duels will be held in the courtyard! Make your way there as soon as possible."

"There is no need to make a spectacle of this," Thessian said.

"What do you mean, Your Grace? Duelling for fun in Redford is as common as the yearly harvest."

Lord Carrell smiled at Thessian. "Follow me, Your Grace. I will find us the best seats."

Somehow, Thessian found himself sitting in the cold, wearing a fur coat made out of ice wolf pelts. He looked at Sir Ian who was standing in the centre of the courtyard, across from Lady Helga.

Lady Helga rested a large double-headed axe over her right shoulder. She lifted it into the air to the cheers of the soldiers and servants.

Sir Ian glanced at Thessian as of asking if it was alright for him to fight a woman.

"No killing," Thessian mouthed to his subordinate.

Sir Ian nodded and focused on his opponent.

Once Lord Fournier announced the start of the duel, Helga launched her attack. She swung her axe wildly around as if it weighed nothing. Her leg movements were lacking in comparison to her strength.

Ian dodged the swings with ease. His movements continued to speed up while the maiden grew tired from expelling energy non-stop.

When Helga paused long enough to catch her breath, Ian kicked her legs from under her and pointed a dagger at her throat.

"It is Sir Ian's win," Lord Fournier shouted with a hint of disappointment.

Next, Lady Elga came out of the crowd with a shortbow. She waited for the start of the match and began firing at her opponent at short intervals. One of the stray arrows ended up flying by Lady Estelle's head.

Lady Estelle grumbled under her breath, "Gods, not this again..."

The crowd got rowdier. They cheered for both sides almost equally.

Elga's eventual downfall was close-range combat. Ian easily overpowered her when she searched her leather quiver for extra arrows.

Compared to the previous two matches, Lady Volga was the only girl who managed to keep pace with Ian. A battle of attrition began when they fought with their daggers at close range. Halfway through the match, Volga changed her weapon to a spear. She kept Ian at a distance and used small knives in between her moves to throw them at him.

One of the knives, whether by fluke or true aim, flew close to Ian's head and pulled on the material of his headscarf. It affected his vision long enough for Volga to point the spearhead at Ian's neck.

"I win!" Volga yelled and punched the air.

Thessian was impressed by her versatility and adaptability during the mock battle. Lady Volga would make a fine addition to his unit with extensive training under Laurence. In a couple of years, she would make a formidable warrior.

"Volga, stop dancing and let your other sisters have a go!" Lord Fournier shouted from his seat.

By the time Lady Volga skipped away, Ian finished adjusting his headscarf. He glanced at Thessian.

"Can you continue?" Thessian mouthed.

Ian nodded and locked his gaze on Lady Taiga who had not changed out of her dress.

She stood next to the ring and raised her hand. "I forfeit. A noble lady should not fight."

Lord Fournier's laughter, along with the rest of the onlookers, filled the courtyard. "What lady? No daughter of mine has gone into the woods and come out without prey. Taiga, get your rapier and get moving."

Taiga pointed her nose upwards. "Papa, I refuse. Let the others act like fools. I will retain my unsullied public image."

Lord Fournier covered his eyes with his hand and waved her away. "Tell Riga to start."

Lady Riga stepped into the ring without a weapon.

Is that child going to forfeit as well?

The ominous sound of a watchtower bell drowned out the excitement for the upcoming duel.

Lord Fournier rose from his seat. "We are under attack. To your stations, men!"

Captain Gagnon arrived promptly and bowed to Lord Fournier. "My Lord, the number of ice wolves coming this way is estimated to be almost fifty. They appear to be led by the Grey Wolf."

Lord Fournier rubbed his hands together. "Get my axe and armour ready."

From Thessian's experience, fifty ice wolves were equal in strength to five hundred men. Though, he knew nothing about the

Grey Wolf the captain mentioned. The nobles he had dined with not long ago were in danger. They could lose many lives in such a battle. "Lord Fournier," Thessian began, rising from the bench, "I will join you."

Lord Fournier grinned. "Ha-ha, I knew you could not resist the pull of a battle."

Lord Carrell arrived shortly after. He had the same calculating look on his face as last night. "I will escort the lords to safety and join you later."

Lord Fournier slapped Lord Carrell on the back, making him almost lose his balance. "Leave the fighting to us. There is no need for you to push yourself."

"My arm will be fine even after killing a few ice wolves, Edgar," Lord Carrell retorted.

Lord Fournier stroked his thick brown beard. "Do as you like." He turned towards Thessian. "I will have armour prepared for you, Your Grace. You are also free to choose any weapon from my collection."

"Thank you, but I already have my sword." Out of the corner of his eye, Thessian noticed Sir Ian approaching. He pulled Sir Ian to one side. "Get to the high ground on the battlements and help Lord Fournier's men."

"What about your safety, Your Highness?"

"I will be fine."

In a flow of soldiers, Thessian and Lord Fournier headed to the front gate of Redford. From the ground, Thessian could see the townsfolk holding bows as if they had practised the drill a million times. They received their orders and, in an orderly fashion, left for their assignments.

Watching a seasoned warrior and commander such as Lord Fournier was a great experience. Thessian could easily see trust and loyalty reflected in the eyes of his soldiers and commoners alike. Joining forces with such a man was the correct decision.

Once the soldiers were assigned their stations, in case the monsters got into the town, Lord Fournier made his way to the battlements to oversee the situation beyond the stone walls.

Thessian spied a large pack of ice wolves waiting in a column formation on a hilltop. He rubbed his eyes for he could not believe their size. Each wolf was equal to a horse. Not only that, ice wolves using military tactics was unheard of. No one back at camp would believe him.

"I have never seen wolves that big," Thessian admitted. "Is that common in these parts?"

Lord Fournier replied, "They have changed over the past two years. Whatever they are eating in those mountains, it would do wonders for our crops."

"This matter is worth investigating."

"Look at you, Your Grace, already acting like the true leader of the land." He pointed to a tall figure standing at the centre of the wolf pack. The figure was easy to miss amidst the large beasts. "That is the Grey Wolf."

Thessian squinted. The figure appeared to be a rather tall, brawny man covered from head to toe in animal pelts that were stitched together. His head was hidden under a hood. "Is Grey Wolf a man? Can he control the ice wolves?"

"He is no man, I assure you." Lord Fournier spat on the ground. "That beast has mercilessly killed ten of my men in the past three months. I suspect he is some kind of evil mage with mind-controlling ability."

"Why would a mage go out of their way to attack your town?"

"Who knows? Perhaps he lost his mind from being in the Hollow Mountains with the monsters for too long."

A powerful roar from the Grey Wolf caused the rest of the ice wolves to advance.

Why did his roar sound so agonized? Thessian looked at the soldiers around him. No one else seemed to have noticed.

Lord Fournier raised his hand. "Archers, prepare to fire on my command!"

The anticipation of battle made every second seem like it lasted a whole minute. The tips of the arrows were dipped in oil and lit with torches. Then, the straining sound of archers pulling back the bowstrings filled Thessian's ears.

The ice wolves passed the one-hundred feet mark, and Lord Fournier shouted, "Fire!"

A rain of arrows flew across the sky like falling meteorites. The first three rows of the wolves were hit, but they remained standing.

Another inhuman roar came from the Grey Wolf, and the ice wolves picked up the pace and split into two columns. One group ate away at the remaining distance to the town's defence wall faster than the archers had the time to reload. The others ran off to the right.

"Get out of the way!"

As a large group of archers ducked, a huge ball of fire blew past their heads, swooping down to strike the ice wolves. Five of them were killed instantly.

Thessian stared at the charred remains of the beasts. He turned his head to find the source of the magical attack.

Standing all alone below the battlements, as if nothing had happened, was Lady Riga.

She smiled at Thessian and lifted her small hands into the air. Another ball of fire began to form above her head.

The soldiers nearby scrambled as far away as they could, muttering curses as they went.

"Your youngest daughter is a mage?" Thessian asked Lord Fournier.

"Did she not say that during her introduction?"

"I do not see how I could connect 'playing with fire' to creating fireballs the size of a fully grown troll."

Lord Fournier chuckled. "I see your point." His expression grew serious once more when the wolves arrived at the base of the walls and began to climb on top of each other. "Pour pitch!"

The soldiers tipped over large vats of boiling, flammable black resin onto the clambering wolves. The animals yowled and cried as their fur burned and their flesh melted away.

Thessian had participated in plenty of siege fights. He still could not get used to the stench of burning flesh.

The Grey Wolf remained a safe distance away, farther than the arrows could reach while observing the situation. He remained perfectly still as if the deaths of his wolves meant nothing to him.

"The second group of wolves is probably going after the rear of the town," Thessian said.

"Lord Carrell, Captain Gagnon, and my daughters are there. There is no need to worry." He whipped out his battle axe and, in one swing, cut down the wolf that managed to climb to the top of the battlements. Its huge head came off its shoulders and rolled in front of Thessian's boots. "Consider it a souvenir for you to take home, Your Grace."

Thessian pulled out his longsword. He plunged the blade deep into the throat of the second wolf. Blood ran down the blade and dripped onto the ground. He yanked his sword out and used as much strength as he could muster to sever the head with one swing.

The wolf's head rolled towards Lord Fournier while the body fell limp to one side. "Consider this one a present from me, Lord Fournier."

They smirked at each other like two naughty youths.

"The one who kills the most gets the best pelt!" Lord Fournier said.

"It is a deal!"

"What about me?" Lady Riga came over and eyed them. "I want to participate in the bet as well."

Lord Fournier placed a hand on his daughter's small shoulder. "This is a man's bet."

She rolled her eyes. "You are only saying that because you know I will win."

"That too," Lord Fournier admitted with a laugh.

Killing seven wolves one after another had Thessian panting.

The beasts became more ferocious as they scaled the walls. They did not seem deterred by the death of their comrades or arrows that were buried in their sides and limbs. If he did not know better, he would have thought they were rabid. Their sharp claws cut the soldiers' armour like butter and their strong jaws broke people in half. Yet, despite the losses Lord Fournier's men suffered, they kept going. Not one deserted their posts.

Amidst the chaos of battle, Thessian spotted Lord Fournier in the street below, fending off an attack from two wolves that had cornered a handful of wounded soldiers. The Lord was grinning, so Thessian proceeded to assess the movements of the enemy.

The Grey Wolf had not moved an inch as if expecting them to come to him.

Thessian accepted the invitation gladly. "Lord Fournier, I will go after the Grey Wolf."

"Your Grace, that man is too dangerous! What if you fall under his spell?"

Mind control was powerful magic forbidden in Hellion. Any mage possessing it was executed, no matter their age. The same happened to necromancers. Raising the dead was considered taboo by the Church of the Holy Light. To combat magic influence, Thessian's father commissioned several amulets to be crafted by the Mage Assembly to protect the imperial family.

"I will be careful," Thessian shouted back.

"I will protect our guest, Papa," Lady Riga notified her father.

Lord Fournier lost his attention to the wolves once more.

Thessian glanced at the child beside him. He did not wish to drag her into battle. She would be safer in the castle.

"Your Grace, the Grey Wolf must have sensed your intentions." She pointed at their enemy. "He is making his way to the forest."

He had no time to sugar-coat his words. "It would be best if you stay here, Lady Riga. You could die out there."

She looked at him with much determination, unsuited for a child her age. "I am a Fournier, Your Grace. We fight or we die fighting."

Somehow, hearing her say those words squeezed his heart. A child her age should be attending tea parties with other ladies or learning an art. Wasn't protecting the happiness and innocence of children part of being a warrior? "I never thought I would hear a twelve-year-old say that to me."

"We must hurry!" She sped down the steps.

Thessian had no time to think or devise a strategy. He heard the Grey Wolf's animalistic roar that startled the creatures of the forest. The young lady was in terrible danger.

He cussed under his breath and chased after her.

TO BE CONTINUED ...

ABOUT THE AUTHOR

May Freighter is an award-winning, internationally bestselling author from Ireland. She writes Fantasy, Urban Fantasy, Paranormal Romance, and Sci-Fi Mysteries that will keep you entertained, mystified, and hopefully craving more. Currently, she's attempting to parent two little monsters and hasn't slept in over 4 years.

Who needs sleep these days, anyway?

On days when May can join her fictional characters on an adventure, stars must align in the sky and meteors will probably rain down. So, keep an eye out.

Her hobbies are photography, drawing, plotting different ways of characters' demise, and picking up toys after her kids. Not exactly in that order, either.

For more information about the author and their work, visit their website: www.authormayfreighter.com

FIND OUT WHAT HAPPENS NEXT IN:

Prince Thessian needs to strengthen the bonds with his allies in the Dante Kingdom, especially if he plans to protect his strong-willed regent. Life would be much simpler if his subordinates could stay out of trouble, and the criminal he's after didn't make him doubt his family.

Meanwhile, Emilia is plagued with nightmares and feels she can't go on if she loses any of her dear friends. In a game of chess, pawns need to be sacrificed, but Emilia isn't used to others giving their lives for her.

With powerful mages crawling out of the woodwork and well-kept secrets that could shake the foundation of the continent, Emilia is certain she has deviated the main plot.

What will she and Thessian sacrifice for the greater good?

Printed in Great Britain
by Amazon

e92586b9-59e5-48c5-b6e3-8cacc4772bd4R01